THE AWESOME ADVENTURES OF

PICKLE BOY

JACK BEE

Cover illustration by Jim Barbero

Edited by ZRB Editing
zrbediting@yahoo.com

DEDICATIONS & ACKNOWLEDGEMENTS

Thanks goes to my wife, for her constant encouragement, to my kids, for being a receptive audience, and to Benjy and Yowi for all their help and friendship. Finally, I cannot leave out all those kids who heard the Pickle Boy stories throughout the years and were wild enough about them to encourage me to write them down. Well, I have finally done it! Hope you enjoy!

ISBN-13: 978-1482577631

PROLOGUE 1

CHAPTER 1 - IN THE BEGINNING 5

CHAPTER 2 – BRAIN FLOOD 21

CHAPTER 3 – DANNY GOES FORTH 59

CHAPTER 4 – TRIALS AND TROUBLES 85

CHAPTER 5 – THERE'S ALWAYS A PRICE TO PAY 106

CHAPTER 6 – A HERO IS BORN 117

CHAPTER 7 – THE COVER COMES OFF 134

CHAPTER 8 – ENEMIES REVEALED 171

CHAPTER 9 – NIGHTMARE SCENARIO 191

CHAPTER 10 – EPIC CONFRONTATION 212

CHAPTER 11 – STILL ALIVE? 226

EPILOGUE – AND REVELATIONS 232

The adventure begins….

PROLOGUE

It was absolutely mortifying that Tommy's parents still considered him a baby. Even though they would only be gone for a few hours, they insisted on getting him a "babysitter". Well, at least it wasn't some annoying teenage girl. Uncle Dan had been recruited for the job this time.

Uncle Dan was pretty cool, and he usually let Tommy stay up as late as he wanted. This time was different. Uncle Dan had offered to tell him a story if he got into bed early. Not the book kind of story, though. This was a little bit weird.

"So, how old are you now, Tommy?" Uncle Dan asked.

"I'm almost ten."

"Well, I have this really good story I could tell you. I haven't told it to you yet because I didn't think you were old enough. In fact, I haven't ever told it to anyone else, either. It's not in a book, though. You just listen to it."

Tommy was skeptical. He had never heard of a story that wasn't in a book.

"Can't you just read me a book instead?" Tommy asked. "I have this dinosaur book that I like, but I don't know all the words in it. Maybe you can read it to me?"

"Just because it's not in a book doesn't mean it's not a good story," said Uncle Dan. "It's about a boy just a few years older than you, and some interesting things happen to him. Very, very interesting things, actually. Tell you what. Listen to the story for a little bit, and if you don't like it, I'll help you with your dinosaur book."

"Is it scary? Does anybody die in the story?"

"Maybe. You'll just have to find out, Tommy," Uncle Dan replied.

"Ok, if you insist," Tommy frowned. "I don't think I'll like the story, anyway. It's probably really boring. And if it's not in a book there won't be any pictures, either."

"You can make the pictures in your mind, Tommy. It'll be fun, you'll see," replied Uncle Dan.

Tommy shrugged, halfheartedly.

And so, Uncle Dan stood up and began his story, pacing slowly back and forth as he spoke.

The prisoner was led out into the clearing in the middle of the stronghold. He had a scraggly grayish-white beard and was very thin, almost gaunt. For nearly twenty years, the only open air he had enjoyed was his daily hour in the grim fortress courtyard. Tall gray walls surrounded the enclosure, and armed guards, dressed from head to toe in severe, dark grey clothing, patrolled the wall-tops. The two similarly dressed men who had escorted him out of his cell released his arms and permitted him to hobble over to a small stone bench, the only object in the otherwise empty space. He sat down wearily. Within seconds, a small flock of gray pigeons surrounded him. The prisoner reached into his pants pocket and pulled out some bread crumbs.

One of the prisoner's handlers remarked to the other, "Just look at that old fool. Feeding his stupid birds. He even talks to them sometimes. Twenty years, the same thing every day. Why doesn't he just tell the boss what he wants to know so he can go home?"

The other guard waved his right hand dismissively. "You and I both know that there's no way he's ever getting out of here alive, and I think he realizes this by now. Let him enjoy himself, if it keeps him happy."

The prisoner was too busy to hear this conversation. He was hoping for some news. He would never lose hope. Someday, someone would find his hidden treasure. With any luck, it would be someone who would know how to use it responsibly. That was his only chance of escaping. And the world's only chance to escape the coming threat as well.

He looked at one of the birds. There was no apparent difference between this particular bird and any of the others. After a quick glance back at the guards to see if they were paying him any attention, the prisoner held out a piece of crust. The bird hopped onto his lap.

Bending over to stroke the bird's head, the man whispered, "Anything? Any news at all?"

The bird looked up into the prisoner's face and shook its head negatively.

The prisoner's shoulders drooped, and, with a small sigh, he continued to feed the birds.

No matter what, and no matter how long it took, he must not lose hope.

"Wait a minute," said Tommy. "Uncle Dan, you said you would be telling me a story about a boy. Who is this prisoner? Why are you telling me about him?"

"Hold on, Tommy. You'll find out. Eventually. Have patience, and everything will be clear. The fewer interruptions there are, the more of the story I can tell, ok? Now," continued Uncle Dan, "I'll tell you about the boy."

CHAPTER 1

IN THE BEGINNING

There was once a boy named Danny Green. Danny was a fairly average eleven and a half year old kid who lived in Brooklyn, one of the five boroughs of New York City. It's close enough to Manhattan that on a clear day, you can see the Empire State Building if you look in the right direction and down the right street. Danny was just under five feet tall, of medium build, and had darkish brown hair that his parents made him keep short because he could never remember to brush it. Aside from a light dusting of freckles, there was nothing particularly distinguishing about Danny's features, which suited him just fine. Danny had a six year old sister named Miri, whom everyone (besides Danny) thought was the most adorable thing in the universe. She actually wasn't that bad as far as sisters go, but the little princess, with her brunette ponytail and deep dimples, sure got lots of attention. Miri also had an irritating tendency to follow him around, especially when his friends came over, which was kind of annoying.

Like his son, Danny's father was not one who would stand out in a crowd. Mr. Green was of average height with thinning brown hair, which he usually covered, while in public, with a hat of some kind. Danny's mother was thin and petite, with dark brown shoulder length hair, pretty green eyes and a bubbly laugh. Mr. and Mrs. Green both worked at decent but unglamorous jobs, his father as an accountant in a bank, and his mother as a speech therapist. The Green family lived on the third floor of a six-story apartment building in the Midwood section of Brooklyn. They were not exactly loaded with cash, but they were able to afford the occasional family trip or restaurant night, and Danny was ok with that. Then one day, Danny's parents did something really awesome. They bought a house!

During the summer, while Danny was away at camp, his parents had moved the family out of the building where Danny had lived most of his life into a small but comfortable two-story house on East 13th Street. It wasn't a very new house, and the previous owners had left it quite messy. Danny didn't care. Anything was better than fighting the cockroaches that lived in their apartment building. Living in a house also meant that he would not have to share a bedroom with Miri anymore. It had been a little embarrassing having to be in the same room with all those pink girlie pillows and stuffed ponies, which somehow always managed to end up on his bed.

The worst of the mess was in the basement, and now that Danny was home from camp, it was his job to deal with it. His parents were still very busy setting up their new home, and would be gone most of the day shopping. Miri had been shipped to their grandparents while Danny had the task of clearing out the junk from the not-as-yet air-conditioned basement. Well, at least they trusted him enough to leave him home alone. Resignedly, Danny trooped down the stairs. What a way to spend his last two days of summer vacation!

He had seen the basement before, of course, but he still was amazed at the extent and variety of the trash down there. Danny wasn't the neatest guy himself, but he couldn't imagine how anything could ever get to look this bad. His parents had promised him tickets to see the Mets at Citi Field if he did a good job, but Danny was starting to wonder if it was worth it, especially with the way the Mets were playing lately.

The basement floor was barely visible under the mounds

of junk. Broken pieces of wood, twisted metal bars, old carpet remnants and heaps of plaster were piled high against the walls. The scene reminded Danny of some pictures he'd seen of houses after some hurricane or earthquake – he couldn't remember which – but not exactly. The piles were a little too…orderly. This mess almost looked like someone made it on purpose.

Danny wiped away the sweat that had already begun to form on his forehead, went back upstairs for some old clothes and some water bottles, and got to work. For two hours he went at it non-stop, filling and removing fifteen heavy-duty garbage bags full of assorted trash. Slowly but surely, one of the walls and about a quarter of the basement floor was cleared of debris. Deciding that it was time for a small break, Danny leaned against the one cleared wall and cracked open a bottle of Pure Springs water.

As he gulped down the warm and flat-tasting drink, Danny looked around at the rest of the basement, wondering again how all this stuff ended up there. His imagination began to drift a little. Maybe some secret agents once used the basement as a hideout, and used the piles to disguise the hidden entrances! Or maybe bank robbers buried their stolen cash here under tons of junk! A drop of sweat rolled into his eye, making him blink. Most likely, it was just some old junk collector's gatherings. Danny sighed and shook his head. He had better get back to the job or he would never get finished.

Swallowing the last of his water, Danny absentmindedly drummed his fingers against the wall behind him as he straightened up to return to work. He had taken two steps toward the nearest pile when he felt a slight tremor behind him. He spun around. The wall he had just been leaning against was visibly shaking! A deep rumbling sound, seemingly from behind the wall, followed. Bits of plaster began to flutter down from the ceiling. The stirrings of a good-sized panic bubbled up in the pit of his stomach. He was all alone, and his parents wouldn't be home for hours. What was happening? Could it be an earthquake? He remembered hearing once that those didn't really happen in New York. And it was only the one wall that was shaking. Maybe part of the house was collapsing? Danny backed away from the wall and got ready to run, just in case.

There was some additional rumbling from the wall, and then, to Danny's amazement, a section of the wall began to sink slowly into the ground! Danny backed up a few more steps. He was scared, but also curious. This was definitely not an earthquake or a collapse. The wall was sinking too smoothly for this to be anything but a man – made event. After about thirty seconds, the section had submerged completely into the floor. There was now an empty black rectangle shape in the wall of Danny's basement, almost inviting Danny to discover what lay beyond.

Danny couldn't believe what he had just seen. Some kind of secret door had just opened up in his basement! But what had caused it? Danny thought back to what he had been doing right before he heard the first rumbling. He had tapped his fingers, right next to where the doorway had appeared. It was very likely that this had been the trigger. But why would someone put a sliding wall in his basement? Where, or what, could it lead to? Maybe he was right about the secret agents. Or better yet, the bank robbers! There could be something worth a lot of money back there somewhere! Maybe gold! Or a million dollars! Now more curious than scared, Danny cautiously crept up to the gap in the wall. The air felt cooler here, and a faint, vaguely familiar smell that he couldn't immediately identify wafted from the unknown area. He peered into the empty space, but could not make out anything in the utter darkness. Danny held on to the doorframe with one hand and stretched out the other into the void. He felt nothing. He listened for some sound, perhaps the scurrying of rats or some other creatures (maybe monsters!) but didn't hear anything either.

Minutes passed, as Danny tried to figure out what to do next. He was becoming less and less scared, and more and more curious, about what was behind the basement walls. He thought of waiting for his parents to get home, but he just couldn't wait that long to find out. Stuff like this never happened to regular kids like him. This was like an adventure or something! Maybe he'd become famous! A newspaper headline flashed through Danny's brain:

BROOKLYN BOY FINDS MYSTERIOUS TREASURE

He couldn't pass up this chance. And, he'd be really, really careful.

Uncle Dan stopped for a moment to look at Tommy. Tommy was sitting straight up in his bed with his blanket pulled up around his neck. He did not look bored at all. Smiling to himself, he resumed his slow pacing and continued his tale.

Danny scooted upstairs to the kitchen and grabbed a flashlight. Trembling with excitement, he raced back to the opening in the wall and shone the flashlight inside. The beam revealed a gray stone or cement floor leading out into the distance, but the light did not have enough range to show him how far the path extended. He took a deep breath, glanced behind him once more, then took a hesitant step forward into the darkness. Unknown to him at the time, this was the first step on a path which would change his life forever. There would be times that he wished he had never taken that first step.

He gingerly made his way down the dark corridor. The flashlight beam revealed a downward-sloping tunnel, its bare-earth walls reinforced here and there by cobweb-covered wooden beams. Every so often, Danny glanced back at the square of light that was his "normal" basement, which was getting smaller and smaller as he went on. He had progressed about fifty feet down the hallway when he got a serious case of the creeps. Chills ran up and down his spine. Maybe this wasn't such a good idea, Danny thought. What if the tunnel collapsed? What if the secret opening closed suddenly? No one would even know where to look for him! Danny was just about to turn and run back to the basement when the corridor abruptly ended at a huge wooden door.

Danny played the flashlight over the obstacle in front of him. The massive door was held shut by a thick rusty padlock. This basically meant the end of his grand adventure. Now he'd have to wait until his parents got home to find out what was behind the door. He sure couldn't break that lock by himself! Oh well. It would have been cool to keep the tunnel secret, but now he had no choice if he wanted to know the truth about the basement. He supposed he would have told his parents about it eventually, though. Danny sighed. He was both disappointed and…strangely relieved. There was probably nothing too exciting here anyway. Probably some dumb wine cellar or something just as boring. Frustrated, Danny kicked at the door and turned away.

He had taken two or three steps back up the tunnel when he heard a low-pitched groaning and tearing sound behind him. Danny nearly jumped out of his skin, and with a small scream raced towards the basement as if a horde of horrible creatures were chasing him (which for all he knew, was actually happening). Danny had never run so fast in his life. In just a few seconds, he had covered the entire length of the passageway and stumbled back into the junk-filled room. Frantically, Danny tried to remember the rhythm in which he had been drumming his fingers earlier. He had to get the doorway closed before whatever was down there got out! But it was so hard to think clearly…his hands were trembling and he was gasping for breath, but he closed his eyes and forced himself to concentrate. Danny put his hand on the wall to the right of the doorway and was about to start tapping when he realized that he hadn't heard a sound from the dark passageway since that first unearthly scraping noise. No footsteps, no bumping, no breathing - except his own.

Danny shone the flashlight back into the darkness.

Nothing.

He could do the safe thing and wait until his parents got home. Yep, that's exactly what he should do. Yet he just couldn't bring himself to shut down the secret corridor just yet. He peered into the dark area again, then turned his ear towards it. Still nothing. Danny flicked the flashlight beam down the hallway a few more times, trying to decide what to do. Finally, he breathed deeply, summoned all of his courage, and once again slowly entered the blackness.

He made it all the way back to the wooden door before he discovered what had caused the noise. The large door was now slightly ajar, and the lock was on the floor next to it, still looped through its hinge. The metal of the hinge was almost completely rusted through, and Danny's kick had shaken the door just enough to cause the hinge to fall off, allowing the door to creak open. Well, well. It looks like the mission is back on, Danny thought. He wasn't sure yet if he was happy about this or not.

Danny stretched out his foot to nudge the door open wider. A gust of cool, dusty air hit him in the face, making him cough. That familiar odor that he had gotten a whiff of earlier was much stronger now. The beam of the flashlight through the doorway revealed a small, seemingly empty room, with the same earthen walls as the hallway. This was very disappointing. All this drama for an empty room? It just didn't make sense. Puzzled, Danny stepped forward. The old, beat-up Nikes he had put on for the cleanup job caught on something in the floor and suddenly he was falling, the light flying out of his hand. With a sickening crack, the flashlight slammed into a wall and went dead.

Danny was now in complete darkness. Panic built quickly as he frantically squinted into the gloom, trying to figure out where the door was. He began scrabbling in the dirt floor in front of him, feeling his way along, when his groping fingers bumped into something solid on the floor. Instinctively he pulled at it, and much to his surprise, a section of the floor came up in his hands! Danny tumbled backwards, grasping what felt like a piece of wood to his chest. As he scrambled to get to his feet, he realized that the room was a little less dark now. A faint greenish light was oozing from a square shaped hole in the floor, allowing Danny to make out some of his surroundings.

The cubically shaped room was now partially illuminated by the spooky glow emanating from the opening in the ground. The weird green light made Danny uneasy, but with his flashlight gone, the trip back to the basement made him just as nervous as remaining where he was. At least here he could see his surroundings - but what was making that glow? What in the world had he gotten himself into?

Danny inched over to the hole and peered in. A steep set of stone stairs led further into the ground, and the light seemed brighter near the bottom.

Well, he had come too far to stop now, thought Danny. He was scared, but was also determined to see what lay at the end of all this. Besides, nothing actually dangerous had happened so far, and whatever was here had been locked away for a long time.

There probably wasn't going to be anything down there that would try to take a bite out of him, he reasoned. Semi-convinced, Danny began to descend.

About fifteen damp and slippery steps later, Danny emerged into a low-ceilinged room full of wooden barrels. The room was rectangular and surprisingly large. There were several rows of the barrels, and each barrel was bigger than he was. The smell was stronger than ever now, and Danny finally recognized it. Pickles. Sour pickles, to be exact. His favorite kind!

Wait a minute.

SOUR PICKLES??

Was that what was in those barrels? Why would someone go to all the trouble of building secret walls and passageways just for some pickles?

Danny approached the nearest barrel. It was about twice his height, and felt cool and damp to the touch. There was also a little faucet stuck into the side. He grasped the faucet's handle and gave it a twist. There was some resistance, but with some effort and a rusty squeak, a small drop of clear liquid appeared in the mouth of the faucet, where it hung suspended, as if waiting. Almost reflexively, Danny touched the hanging drop and brought his finger to his mouth.

Well, it definitely tasted like pickles, although the strong tingly sensation that filled his mouth made Danny wonder if they were a little spoiled after all these years. His head also felt a little funny – not dizzy or anything like that, just a little weird. The feeling quickly passed, though, and Danny was left wondering again, why. Why all this trouble, just for pickles? Maybe they were very special, award winning pickles? Who knew? Well, at least he had a cool place to show off to his friends. Maybe they could make some kind of secret clubhouse down here. No longer afraid of his new house's mysteries, Danny decided to poke around and explore a little more.

Mr. and Mrs. Green were on a very, very long line at the local ShopSmart. It was their third store of the day, and Mr. Green was developing a pounding headache as he tried to keep track of their two overflowing shopping carts. Like most men, he enjoyed shopping about as much as going to the dentist. To make matters worse, the elderly woman just in front of them in the line had just pulled out a large handbag practically bursting with coupons, and by the expression on her face, it was apparent that she meant to take advantage of every one of them. He looked over at his wife, who was happily chatting with the woman on line right behind them, although they had just met. Well, at least someone was having fun. Needing a break, Mr. Green excused himself and went outside for some fresh air.

As he strolled through the parking lot, Mr. Green thought back to the moment he had seen the inside of their recently purchased home for the first time. The asking price on the house had been surprisingly low, but once he and his wife had gotten a look at it, they had understood why. While the two-story, single-family home, with stucco siding on the upper floor topping a brick-covered ground floor, was standard for the neighborhood, there were some quite noticeable differences that became apparent upon closer examination. First, there was the address. 1313 East 13th Street. It was enough to give pause to even the most non-superstitious person. Then there was the interior. It seemed that almost every room had several holes in its walls, the floors were all ripped up, and the basement had been filled with the biggest indoor pile of junk that he had ever seen. However, it was the only house the Greens could afford, so they had made the purchase and spent the entire summer making it livable. It was far from perfect, but it would do for now.

The real estate agent who had shown them around had apologized for the condition the house had been in, claiming that the previous owner had been a little bit of an oddball, some kind of crazy scientist, who had not been seen for many years. No one really knew much about him, but there were various stories floating around the neighborhood – that he had been involved in an unpleasant family disagreement, that he had some kind of treasure or some secret invention – all sorts of wild gossip. The agent had also mentioned one of the crazier rumors he had heard. Using an exaggerated spooky voice, the agent had cracked that it was possible that the house looked like this because someone had been searching for something hidden there, possibly something dangerous. However, this was quickly dismissed as a silly theory that some of the guys at the real estate office had been tossing around. "Hey – maybe it's not a good idea to leave children alone in the house, huh?" the agent had chuckled.

Mrs. Green had not been in the room at the time, and Danny's father had never bothered to repeat it to her, as he didn't want his wife to get all worried over some dumb real estate agent joke. She had been weirded out enough by the address alone. Still, the more he thought about the way the house had looked back then, the less funny the real estate agent's comment now seemed. There *had* been something a little suspicious about the house's condition – and that, together with the extremely reduced asking price, was making him more nervous the more he thought about it. The real estate people must have been having a hard time finding someone to buy it. Could it be that in his excitement in finding something affordable, he hadn't properly considered what they were purchasing? Maybe those real estate people knew more than they were telling! A large lump started to form in Mr. Green's throat.

Inside, Mrs. Green had finally reached second place on the checkout line. The coupon lady had just completed the excruciatingly slow and careful task of loading her purchases onto the counter when Mr. Green hurried up to his wife with a worried look on his face and whispered, "Is it going to be much longer, Aliza?"

"What's the matter, Jack? Is something wrong?"

"Well, it's probably nothing, but, um, when we were looking at the house, the real estate guy mentioned something to me while you were in another room. Just some silly rumor he once heard, probably nonsense, about something that may have been hidden in the house at one point…"

Mrs. Green's face turned pale. "What are you saying? Who hid what in our house? Why didn't you say anything to me?"

"Well, the guy said it was probably nothing, but he sort of joked about making sure kids aren't left alone for too long…"

"Ohmygosh! Danny!" exclaimed Mrs. Green, whipping out her cell phone.

The answering machine went on after four rings. Mr. Green, seeing the worry in his wife's expression, tried to keep his voice steady. "He probably can't hear the phone ring from the basement. Look, let's just finish up here and drop our stuff off at the house. We'll check on Danny and go back out to finish the shopping. I'm sure it's nothing," he repeated nervously. He glanced anxiously towards the front of the line, where the coupon lady was arguing with the annoyed-looking checkout girl, and tried to calm himself down.

The setting seemed unreal, almost dreamlike, to Danny as he wandered among the barrels. There sure were a lot of them. He counted seven rows of barrels before he got to the far wall of the room, and there were ten barrels in each row. Danny wondered how full the barrels were. Well, only one way to find out. He braced himself against the back wall and put one foot on the faucet of the nearest barrel. Springing upwards, he grabbed the lip of the barrel with both hands and scrambled onto the top.

Danny had to crouch here due to the closeness of the ceiling, as he gazed out at the rows of barrels stretching out in front of him. He noticed that the covers of the barrels had handles set into them. Danny leaned over to the barrel next to the one he was on, grabbed the handle set in its top, and yanked. With a hiss of escaping air and a powerful whiff of sour pickles, the cover shifted upwards. He pulled a little more, and to his great surprise, the whole cover popped free suddenly, causing him to lose his balance! Arms spinning wildly, Danny belly-flopped right into the open barrel.

Danny ended up completely submerged for a second or two before he resurfaced, coughing and kicking his legs madly as he tried to keep his head out of the pickle juice. He eventually managed to wade over to the side, where he was able to grasp the top of the barrel and pull himself out.

Danny dropped to the basement floor. He was dripping pickle juice all over the place, and his sneakers made wet squishy sounds as he walked back to the stone steps. Yuck! Now he was a real mess. He smelled like a sour pickle. His clothes – Danny couldn't be sure in this light, but it seemed that his clothes were turning green! How was he going to explain this to his parents? He had better clean up fast or his little secret adventure would not be secret for too long. With a last look back at his strange discovery, Danny headed up the stairs and back towards home.

As he headed back down the hallway, Danny was struck by the realization that his legs hadn't felt any actual pickles when they were kicking around in the barrel. There was just the juice, all the way down! This was just getting stranger and stranger.

Danny entered the "normal" part of his basement more confused than excited about his little adventure. It was cool to have a secret room in his basement, but what nut would go to all that trouble just to hide some pickle juice? Danny looked at the opening in the wall again. Should he tell his parents? They would probably get all worried and not let him in there anymore. Grownups always seemed to get too worried about things. Danny sighed and stepped up to the wall. If this didn't work, his parents would find out in any case. He tapped out the same rhythm he had used earlier, and with little fanfare, the wall moved back into place with a low grinding noise. The secret was safe, at least for now.

Danny went upstairs to his room to get some new clothes. The ones that he was wearing now had turned an even deeper shade of green, and had also gotten very sticky from his bath in the pickle juice. In fact, they were so sticky that when he tried to pull his t-shirt over his head, he found that all his clothing seemed to be stuck together! His shirt wouldn't come off because it was stuck to his pants, which were in turn somehow attached to his socks and sneakers. He also found that his clothing had somehow become both more elastic and resilient, sort of like the rubber snow boots he always struggled to stretch over his shoes. After much yanking and twisting, he finally had some success by pulling his arms out of his sleeves and then unrolling the mass of green garments down his body. It was like unpeeling an unripe banana. When he reached his sneakers, he was able to stretch the fabric enough to yank his feet out of them, after which he rolled the whole green mess into a ball and threw it under his bed, far enough to avoid his mother's built-in dirty clothing radar. Danny then ran down the hallway to the bathroom, hoping that a good shower would get rid of the pickle smell.

Twenty minutes later, while Danny was getting dressed, the front door banged open. "Danny!" his father yelled. "Where are you? Are you ok?"

Mr. Green anxiously ran through the first floor to the landing that led to the basement steps. How could he have left Danny alone? He could never forgive himself if anything had happened to him. He rushed down the stairs, fearing the worst. "Danny!" he shouted again, as he reached the bottom. His son was nowhere to be found. Mr. Green anxiously scanned the basement. It appeared rather harmless. In fact, it seemed that Danny had actually made some decent progress towards the cleanup project.

"Hi, Dad," came a voice from behind him.

Mr. Green gave a little startled jump and turned around. "Danny! There you are!" Danny's father gave his son a harder-than-usual hug, then stepped back to examine him. "Well, Danny. You seem all right. Thank G-d. Uh, hey, that's some pretty good work you did around here," he remarked, gesturing around the basement. "Listen, just out of curiosity, you didn't see anything odd or maybe dangerous while you were down here, did you?"

Danny had always tried very hard to tell the truth, especially to his parents, but he really wanted to keep his discovery secret, at least for another day or two. So, choosing his words carefully, he put on his most innocent look and replied, "No, Dad, nothing "dangerous". Why do you ask?"

"Well, I heard some rumors about the people who lived here before us. They had a reputation for being… well, kind of different. It's probably nothing to worry about, but I want your word that if you see or smell anything peculiar, you'll tell me right away." Danny's father took another quick scan of the basement, scratching his head as he did.

Without waiting for Danny to answer (for which Danny

was very happy, as he didn't want to make that promise), his father continued, "Ok, I'm going back out. We should be home for good in another hour or two. Just be careful. Say, did you bring any pickles down here? It smells like pickles a little. Mr. Green took a few curious sniffs as Danny held his breath, then shook his head. "Well, never mind. See you later, son!"

Danny did some more work in the basement that afternoon, but did not feel compelled to re-visit the room full of barrels that day, or even the next. He was really busy getting ready for school and helping his parents around the house. Added to that was the fact that the thrill of his big find had mostly worn off. What was there about a room full of pickle juice to get excited about? He wasn't even sure why he was keeping it a secret from his parents. He supposed he would tell them eventually, when the right time came around.

"Well, that's all for tonight, Tommy," said Uncle Dan.

"Hey, you can't stop now! What about the pickle juice? Who put it there? Who lived there before Danny? What about..."

"Tommy, Tommy. It's late. Next time we'll start earlier and I'll be able to tell you more. But right now it's time to go to bed."

"Aww, come on, Uncle Dan!"

"Sorry. Now, you be good, or your parents won't let me come anymore to babysit. Good night, Tommy."

Uncle Dan closed the door (but not all the way) and left. Tommy lay in bed for a while, thinking about the story. Eventually he drifted off to sleep.

CHAPTER 2

BRAIN FLOOD

It was just two nights later that Tommy's father got some great tickets for a Broadway show. The only reason he was hesitant to use them was Tommy, who generally was not happy with being left with a babysitter. However, Tommy didn't seem to mind at all when he was informed that Uncle Dan would be coming to watch him again. In fact, on the night of the show, Tommy got ready for bed quickly without even being told. He made sure that all his homework was done, his teeth brushed, and his room all cleaned up so he would be ready when Uncle Dan came. His parents had never seen anything like it. He even got a little impatient when his mother spent too long putting on her makeup. Finally, his parents were gone. Tommy dragged Uncle Dan up the stairs to his room to continue the story, and true to his word, Uncle Dan spent almost an hour continuing the adventures of Danny Green.

Tuesday, the sixth of September, 2011, otherwise known as the first day of the school year, arrived all too soon. It was a busy morning in the Green household. Mrs. Green had grabbed some coffee and had gone out to the garage to get the car. Miri, who had prepared her small pink backpack weeks in advance, was in the bathroom, brushing her hair. Danny was still scrambling around for some pens, notebook paper and, of course, a snack to take for recess. As he passed by the door to the basement, an urge for the taste of sour pickles struck him. The fact that there were no actual pickles in the barrels was not an issue – the juice would be just fine. Luckily, his keychain was equipped with a small but powerful LED flashlight. He would have to be fast. The last thing he needed was for his nosy sister to discover his secret.

Danny grabbed an empty water bottle someone had left on the kitchen counter and hurried downstairs. He tapped out the correct sequence in the right spot and fished out his flashlight as he waited impatiently for the secret wall section to descend. Danny charged through the dusty hallway beyond, through the open rusty door, and down the stairs to the subbasement with the weird green light. Turning the tap on the first barrel of pickle juice, Danny filled his water bottle to the top. Then he ran back up the stairs, back down the hallway to the regular basement area, and tapped the wall next to the opening. The wall made its usual low rumbling as it closed up. Danny could hear his mother honking the horn, and as he turned to dash upstairs, he almost ran right over Miri.

"Hey! Watch out, Danny!"

"Whoa! Sorry, Miri. I didn't know you were there. Um, when did you come downstairs?" Danny asked nervously.

"I just came down now to see if you were ready. What were you doing?"

"Uhh...nothing. Just checking on something," Danny answered. He brushed past Miri and headed upstairs before Miri could ask any more questions. It seemed like his secret was safe for now...

"Danny, why was the wall moving?" chirped Miri, in a sweet, innocent voice.

Danny tripped on the top stair and went sprawling. "What are you talking about, Miri?" blurted Danny as he picked himself up. "What wall? Stop making up crazy stuff!" He tried to sound annoyed, as if the very idea of a wall moving was preposterous. He kept his back turned to his sister so that she wouldn't see the alarmed expression on his face. "Come on! Mom's waiting for us!"

Danny rushed out to the car before she could reply. How could he have been so careless? He wasn't worried Miri would find the secret door. The chance of her tapping on the wall in the correct pattern was very small. But what if Miri mentioned something to his parents? They already had suspicions about the basement. Maybe they wouldn't let him go down there by himself anymore! Well, he would just have to deal with whatever happened. Hopefully, Miri would just forget about it, as little kids tend to do.

Miri followed him out to the car and climbed into her car seat. As she settled in, she whispered, "I didn't imagining it. Nuh-uh. Danny's just a meanie. Reeeeeally." Miri pouted and stuck her tongue out at Danny, who pretended not to notice.

"Whatever," muttered Danny. Little sisters sure were a pain sometimes.

The all-boys school that Danny attended had a huge paved yard in front where all the students would gather before classes. On the first day of the school year, the principal, a short, balding and somewhat nervous man named Mr. Fine, would announce the names of the teachers of each class, followed by the names of the boys in that class. Each grade had two classes. Danny, who was entering the sixth grade, was very concerned about just which kids would end up in his class. For the last three years, he had been together with his best friends, Sammy and Joe. Most of the other boys ranged in personality from nice to somewhat normal, with a small sprinkling of slightly weird, but nobody too nasty or snobbish. And then there was the Big Three. The worst thing in the world was to have to spend a year in the same class as The Big Three.

The Big Three, sometimes abbreviated to just "B3", looked exactly like they sounded – big. There was a good reason for that - they were a year or two older than everyone else in their grade. It was said (though never within the B3's earshot) that they had failed kindergarten, maybe twice, and had to repeat it. Shia Dekel was their leader. He had at least somewhat of a brain, but this just made him more dangerous. Mike Bitowsky was Shia's right hand man, and the biggest and dumbest of them all was known simply as "Ox". The Three used their size to terrorize the boys unlucky enough to share a classroom with them. What made it even worse was that they knew they could get away with anything they wanted. Shia's father was an important and well-respected person, and it was obvious to all of the other students that Mr. Fine would never risk doing anything to get on Mr. Dekel's bad side. Anyone stupid enough to complain to the principal about the Big Three would get the privilege of having Mr. Fine respectfully ask these monsters to say they were sorry and not to do again whatever it was they had done, the Big Three smirking all the while. Later, Ox would "apologize" by delivering a knuckle sandwich or two to the tattletale's stomach. Yep, school was tons of fun for the Big Three's classmates.

Danny usually walked to school, but Danny's mother had a tradition to drive the kids on the first day. Danny just hoped she wouldn't kiss him goodbye in front of all his friends once they arrived. He was getting a little too old for that. He need not have worried, as his mother was running late and dropped him off half a block away from the schoolyard. Danny ambled down the street, the familiar sounds of school signaling the final conclusion of summer.

Inside the yard, boys were wandering around, finding and greeting their friends whom they hadn't seen during the summer. Some of the students, new to the school, just stood around on the side, staying out of everybody's way. As Danny entered the yard, he heard a familiar voice call out,

"Hey, Danny! Over here!"

He turned to see Sam and Joe tossing a football back and forth in the middle of the yard. Joe was a tall and athletic boy with dark brown hair who loved playing sports. He was a serious kid and sort of quiet, but a good friend. Sammy was short and a little chubby with red hair and glasses. Sammy was a big professional baseball fan, and in general would rather follow a sport than play it. He was lots of fun to hang out with, except when he got too obsessed over his favorite team, the New York Mets. The three boys had become best friends in the third grade, during what they had called the Year of Terror, which was the last time the Big Three had been in their class.

Danny's new home was much closer to where Sammy and Joe lived, and they had already decided that they would walk home from school together after Danny's family made their move. It would have been nice if they could have walked to school together as well, but Sammy was the kind of boy who always seemed to be running late, and Danny and Joe tactfully decided to get to school on their own schedule.

Danny hustled over to join his friends.

"Hey, how's it going, guys?" asked Danny. "How was your summer?"

"Not bad, not bad," answered Sammy, while trying to tuck in his shirt.

“Way too short,” said Joe.

“Think we’ll be in the same class again?” said Danny.

“I don’t see why they would change things,” said Joe. “We don’t give them too much trouble. But you never know what Mr. Fine’s got going on in that weird bald head of his.”

“Just as long as we’re not with the Big Three,” Sammy said nervously.

Danny knew that no matter how unpleasant a year with the Big Three would be for him, it would be much worse for Sammy. The Big Three were especially brutal to pudgy kids, especially if they wore glasses, and Sammy’s red hair made him even more of a target. The Year of Terror had cost Sammy four pairs of glasses, all broken “by accident”.

“Oh, come on, Sammy,” said Joe. “Don’t talk about those creeps. You just ruined my mood.”

The boys discussed their summers for a few minutes until the loud feedback of Mr. Fine’s megaphone squawked across the yard.

“Attention, attention. I will now be reading off the teachers and class lists for the school year. When you hear your names, form an orderly line in front of the main entrance. When the entire class has been called, you will be given a room number and proceed to your classroom with one of the school monitors. Your teacher will follow shortly.”

The megaphone gave another nasty squawk. Mr. Fine, thick glasses perched on the end of his thin nose, peered intently at the piece of equipment as if that would somehow solve the problem. Danny heard some mean-sounding laughter from the back of the yard. Sure enough, there was Shia and his gang, with the usual circle of empty space around them.

"Oh, rats!" said Joe. "B3 showed up. I thought they'd be in prison by now!" Joe was trying to talk tough, but Danny could tell that he was worried. "I sure hope our streak continues," Joe added quietly. "I heard some pretty ugly things happened in their class last year."

Soon enough, Mr. Fine was reading off the sixth grade class lists. The first three names that were called out belonged to the Big Three, who decided that this was enough of an accomplishment to high-five each other. The rest of the schoolyard quieted suddenly, as the remaining sixth graders waited to hear their fates.

As the next twenty two names were announced, the expression on that boy's face changed to one of deep dread and apprehension. When Mr. Fine finally signaled the end of the list of doomed boys by announcing their room number, the shouts of relief from the remaining sixth graders rang throughout the schoolyard.

Danny, Joe, and Sammy, along with the other kids whose names had been called, dejectedly formed a line in front of the school's main entrance.

"OK, boys, Room 613 for you. Your homeroom teacher this year is Mr. Brown. Good luck!" said Mr. Fine.

"Yeah, you'll need it!" shouted a loud voice from the back of the yard.

Mr. Fine adjusted his glasses and pretended not to hear.

The Brooklyn Charter School for Boys (commonly referred to by the students as "BCSB") that Danny and his friends attended was structured a little differently from other public schools. Aside from the fact that there were no girls, the school day itself was arranged in a way that minimized movement between classes. More than half of each day was spent in the same classroom (their homeroom) with one teacher who was their "main subjects" teacher. This teacher would teach them most of the core subjects such as math, English, and social studies, while classes such as science and the arts were taught in different rooms in periods scattered throughout the day. The main subjects teacher was usually a very well-rounded educator with an engaging personality. The Board that ran the school hired only the most seasoned and qualified teachers for this all-important and demanding position. Danny didn't know who this mysterious Board was, but any grownup smart enough to realize that boys and girls did not mix well in the classroom was ok by him.

Danny's classmates filed into room 613, which was located on the fourth floor of the school. Other than the Big Three, the class was basically the same as in the previous year, with one or two new boys. Nobody looked very happy as they rushed to find a seat. One of the new kids was a very skinny boy with big glasses and lots of pens in his pocket. He took a seat right in front of the teacher's desk. As Danny passed him, he couldn't help but think that this kid might as well have a target on his back. Shia and his gang would have lots of fun with that poor soul.

Danny chose a seat on the left side of the room against the wall, about three rows back from the teacher's desk. He didn't like sitting too close to the front because he would get called on too often, but also did not like sitting too far back, especially this year. The area in the back of the class was where the Big Three usually set up their base. Joe found a desk one row to his right, and Sammy sat himself right in front of Joe.

The door to the classroom slammed shut with a bang. Everyone turned to the front of the room, expecting their new teacher. What they saw instead was Shia sitting on the teacher's desk, his two goons right behind him.

"Listen up, everybody!" Shia snarled. "There's going to be some new rules this year, so everybody better pay attention. I wouldn't want anybody getting hurt because they didn't know the rules." Mike and Ox made sinister laugh-snorting noises. Shia stood up and began slowly walking around the room, like a lion stalking a group of trapped gazelles. "Me and my friends here have decided to open up a new business. We'd like all of you to be our customers, in fact!"

The room was deathly quiet. Finally the new kid with the pens in his pocket stuttered, "Uh, w-what kind of business?"

Shia smiled wickedly. "I'm glad you asked, punk. It's an insurance business. "The B3 Insurance Company". We're gonna protect you!"

"From what?" asked Pocket-Pens.

Oh no, thought Danny. This kid is in for it now. Danny was too scared to say anything, though.

Shia put his face very close to Pocket Pens. The difference in the two boys' size was very noticeable.

"What's your name, little boy?" Shia asked.

"M-M-Martin," trembled the boy. "Hey! Give those back!"

Shia had deftly plucked Martin's glasses off his nose. "We're gonna protect you from accidents, M-M-M-Martin. Accidents happen all the time. For instance, I accidentally dropped your glasses." Shia let go of the glasses, which clinked off the hard classroom floor. "And," Shia continued, "It is entirely possible that my friend Ox over there might accidentally stomp on them." Ox ambled over and raised a large foot.

"No!!" yelped Martin.

"Hold on, Ox. I think our company may have its first customer. For only five dollars a week, you can join our accident insurance program, and these kinds of things won't happen to you. What do you say, M-M-M-Martin?"

Tears welled up in Martin's eyes. He fished in his pocket for a minute, and came up with two crumpled up bills. "I'll give you the rest tomorrow, I promise! Please give me back my glasses! I can't see anything without them!"

Martin was practically crying when Ox gave him his glasses back. Ox looked disappointed that he didn't get to break anything.

The rest of the boys either looked away uncomfortably or stared down at their desks. Danny felt his ears turn red. He felt bad for Martin, and both embarrassed and ashamed that he was too scared to do anything about it.

Shia began wrapping up his little presentation. "Well, that's how it works. Make sure to bring in your money on time and we'll make sure there are no accidents. Also, Mike here learned how to break fingers over the summer, just in case you think about snitching."

Just then, the classroom door opened and a fortyish man

with sandy brown hair and stylish glasses walked in. "Hi, guys. My name is Mr. Brown. Find your seats and let's get started. We've got lots to do today!"

Shia and his friends smirked at each other, went to the back of the room, and slouched nonchalantly into their seats.

"You guys sure are a quiet bunch!" said Mr. Brown. "The kids were bouncing off the walls in every classroom I passed by. Not that I'm complaining, of course. Anyway," he continued, turning to the board, "our first subject today will be mathematics, where we'll review everyone's favorite subject, long division." The class groaned. Mr. Brown turned back to the class with a smile. "Good, good, you're human after all. It's really not so bad, you know. I've got some neat tricks I can show you that will help a lot." With that, Mr. Brown began his lesson.

The rest of the school day was uneventful, except for Shia and his friends tripping kids as they carried their lunch trays, laughing about all the "accidents" that seemed to be happening. Nobody else thought it was funny. In fact, most kids were frightened out of their wits. As Danny and his friends walked to the city bus stop after school, Joe sputtered, "Can you believe those guys? They're basically telling us that they'll beat us up if we don't pay them off! And they'll probably get away with it, too! That's what bothers me the most!"

"Well, at least if we do pay them they won't bother us," Sammy pointed out.

"Yeah, well, maybe you get an allowance or something, but I don't know where I'm going to come up with that kind of money every week," Joe said angrily.

Danny did not know what to think. He hated the fact that Shia and his gang were able to terrorize everybody without consequences, of course, but at least he was lucky enough to get a five dollar weekly allowance (when he deserved it). He certainly did not want to use it to pay off those bullies, but Shia did imply that whoever paid would be safe. As Danny adjusted the straps on his backpack, he felt the lump made by the bottle of pickle juice, which he had totally forgotten about since that morning. He dug it out to take a quick drink.

"What's that?" asked Sammy. "Some kind of fruit juice? Looks weird. Green? Eww. Kinda gross, Danny!"

"Actually, it's, uh, pickle juice," answered Danny, raising the bottle to his mouth. He took a small gulp and again felt that weird tingly sensation he had felt when he first tasted the stuff in his basement. This time the feeling did not go away after a few seconds, as it had before. His head, or more accurately, his brain, felt odd, different somehow. It was as if his thoughts had always been tangled up, and now he was thinking more clearly than ever. All the colors of the visible spectrum seemed to stand out sharply as he looked around. It was too much to take in all at once. He closed his eyes and dropped to his knees for a few moments, until he felt steady enough to stand up.

Still kneeling, he opened his eyes to find himself face to face with a heavily studded metal belt. The belt held up a pair of worn-looking and scuffed black jeans, which ended in heavy black hiking boots. Danny looked up at the clothes' owner, and a sinking feeling settled in his stomach. The scowling face of a very unpleasant teenage boy sneered down at him. The teenager, who appeared to be about five years older than Danny, was wearing a black t-shirt with the sleeves cut away to expose heavily muscled arms. A tattoo of a sinister-looking man wearing an old-fashioned hat stood out prominently from the boy's right bicep. A lit cigarette was pressed between two of the fingers of his left hand, while the right held a thick wooden baseball bat.

Danny and his friends had forgotten a very important fact of city life since the end of the last school year – that they had to be very careful about the route they took to get home. There was a boarded-up, abandoned-looking apartment building on one side of the street two blocks away from the school. A couple of years earlier, some boys in their class had gotten themselves beaten up by some older kids who liked to hang out in front of the structure. Everyone knew to keep to the other side of the street to stay out of trouble. Unfortunately, all of the events of the first day of school had caused them to lose track of where they were not supposed to go, and they had ended up right in front of the building. The day had just gone from bad to very, very bad.

Danny's mouth went dry with fright. The bottle fell from his trembling hands. Sammy let out a scared squeak behind him. Danny turned to see four more tough-looking teens advancing in a loose semicircle behind them, each grinning nastily. Joe looked over at Danny nervously, pale with fear.

Danny watched, paralyzed, as Joe and Sammy were grabbed and had their arms twisted behind them. Joe managed to maintain composure, but tears were beginning to stream down Sammy's chubby cheeks. The thug holding Sammy said, "Hey, Jack! Look what we caught us!"

The boy dressed in black answered in a cold voice, "I see we caught us a bunch of punk kids who don't know better than to respect our property! I think they need to be taught a lesson. What do you think, guys?"

"Yeah!"

"We'll teach 'em in a way they'll never forget!"

Danny felt tears coming to his eyes as well. He tried his best not to cry, but his quavering voice gave away how scared he was. "Please, we didn't mean to…"

"Shut up, punk!" roared Jack. "You shoulda known better. All you loser school kids are supposed to know that this is BlackJack's turf. That's me, by the way. BlackJack. Because of my favorite color. You disrespected me. Now you're going to pay my price!"

"H-how much d-do you w-w-want?" Danny trembled, tears beginning to flow.

"Oh, we don't accept cash. Credit cards either." BlackJack's gang thought this was hysterical. Jack grinned cruelly. "We take our payment in broken bones. With the Jack of Clubs!" BlackJack flexed his tattoo at the terrified boys. "And you're going to pay first!"

With that, BlackJack lifted his bat and began to swing. Danny had no time to do anything except to raise his arms over his head and close his eyes. Danny's only thought was,

…Please don't let this hurt too much...

There was a loud cracking sound, and then silence. After a few confused seconds, Danny cautiously lowered his arms and opened his eyes. What he saw amazed him.

The great and fearsome BlackJack was standing in front of him, mouth wide open, looking like a total idiot at the remains of his bat. He was still holding the bottom third of his weapon, but the rest of it was in splinters all over the ground. What happened? Danny wondered. Had BlackJack hit him? He hadn't felt a thing!

BlackJack frowned and shook his head. "Hmph. Bat must've had a crack in it or somethin'. Tony, give me your chain. I'm gonna really give it to this kid!"

One of the boys holding Joe had a heavy metal bicycle chain wrapped over his shoulders, which he took off and handed to Jack. Jack grabbed the chain roughly, swung it up high and brought it down viciously on Danny's head.

Danny did not have time to get his arms back up. He squeezed his eyes shut, hoping again that he wouldn't get hurt too badly.

This time there was a loud "SPLINK." Danny heard BlackJack say some very bad words. He opened his eyes to find little pieces of the chain scattered all over the sidewalk.

"Whoa, cool!" said Joe.

"Tony! You made me look like a moron!" BlackJack shouted. "Why did you give me a broken chain?"

"Hey! Whoa!" barked back Tony. "Back off. My chain was perfectly fine until you, um…"

Until he hit me with it, thought Danny. He hit me with a baseball bat and a metal chain and it didn't hurt at all! In fact, I didn't even feel it!

What Danny did feel was the tingling sensation from the pickle juice. It was all over his body now. Hmmm, thought Danny. He had just had his first real drink of that juice. Could that be the cause…and maybe that's why somebody hid it away so carefully…but that was just crazy…?

BlackJack's street-tough voice broke through Danny's

mental detective work. "Forget it, Tony. This kid's not gonna walk away from here telling everyone he made BlackJack look stupid." Jack whipped out a wicked-looking switchblade and flicked it open.

Sammy and Joe gasped in alarm. Even some of BlackJack's gang thought that things were going too far.

"Hey, Jack, come on, put that away!" said Tony. "He's just some little kid. It's not worth it!"

BlackJack, however, was too enraged to listen to anybody at this point. With an animal snarl, he slashed the blade toward Danny's stomach.

With a confidence that he had never felt before in his life, Danny did not close his eyes. This time he wanted to see.

To BlackJack, it felt as if he had rammed the knife into a brick wall. The knife blade broke off its handle from the force of the blow.

"YAHHHHHH!" BlackJack screamed, staggering backwards and holding his injured hand. The street gang looked at each other confusedly. This was not the way that things were supposed to happen. Without realizing it, they released their grips on Sammy and Joe and started backing away.

Danny was still watching BlackJack, who was stumbling around and clutching his hand. A sense of righteous justice came over him. It wasn't fair that regular kids always had to put up with bullies like this. He was sick and tired of being scared and pushed around by bigger, meaner kids. First Shia and his loser friends, and now this self-important goon. He felt his face flush hot with anger. It was time to do something about it. And maybe he could actually do something. The way he felt now, he felt he could do anything.

Danny took two big steps forward until he was right behind BlackJack.

"Hey, BlackJack!" said Danny loudly.

BlackJack turned around, and Danny swung his fist.

Fortunately for BlackJack, Danny did not have much fighting experience, and the punch did not hit him straight on. Still, the glancing blow to the chest sent BlackJack hurtling about ten feet through the air, where he slammed headfirst into a street lamppost. There was a loud "CLANG," and BlackJack's body fell to the ground and lay still.

There was utter silence for about five seconds as Jack's friends tried to digest what they had just witnessed. When a somewhat shocked Danny turned back to face them, though, Tony let out a frightened yelp.

"Uh, guys, I just remembered a dentist appointment I have," he blurted, before turning and running as fast as he could. The rest of BlackJack's posse followed right behind him.

Danny felt the flush recede from his face as he watched the gang make their escape. That sure sense of righteousness was dissipating as well, now that the heat of the fight was over. Ok, what had just happened? he thought to himself. Was it really the pickle juice? What did it do to him?

"Uh, Danny?" asked Sammy. "Hello? What was that? Did you learn karate or something over the summer?"

"That was no karate, Sammy," exclaimed Joe. "Karate doesn't protect you from baseball bats, and especially knives.

And you can't punch someone across the street, either. How on earth did you do that?" he asked Danny.

"I-I don't know," replied Danny. "I've never done anything like this before." He picked up the bottle of pickle juice, which lay among the bat splinters and chain pieces. He still felt that tingling sensation that had begun when he drank the stuff earlier. If the juice truly was responsible for what he had just been able to do, there was a very good reason why it had been hidden away. But who had put it in his basement? How long ago? There were so many questions…

Joe saw Danny staring intently at the juice bottle and his eye flashed with understanding. "Where exactly did you get that juice, Danny?" he asked. "Didn't you drink that right before that gang ambushed us?

"Yeah, I guess so, but…"

Danny could not believe that Joe had figured it out so quickly. Maybe he should lie and make up some excuse. It was his secret, after all. What good is a secret if everyone knows about it? But then again, it would be nice to have someone to talk to, and these were his best buddies. They shared everything. When any one of them had a problem, they knew they could discuss it with the others. Sammy's parents argued all the time, with each other and with Sammy's crazy older brother, and it made Sammy feel better knowing he could unload to his friends. Joe knew he could complain about his parents' always worrying about money, and it made him feel better knowing his friends would listen. Then there was the time that Danny had thrown a baseball through Joe's parents' bedroom window. Joe had taken the blame and never told anyone who had really done it. Danny made a quick decision to trust his friends and hope for the best.

"Well, I'll tell you guys what I know, but you have to

promise never to say a word to anyone. Let's get out of here. I'll fill you in on the way."

Sam and Joe, with a new kind of respect for their longtime friend, followed Danny as he turned and headed homeward. As they walked, Danny related everything that had happened to him on the day he found the pickle juice. He finished his tale fifteen minutes later, as they arrived at the corner of East 13th Street and Avenue M. The boys stood huddled together on Danny's corner for a few minutes, digesting what Danny had told them.

"So you think this stuff is what let you do what you did today?" asked Joe.

"Who knows? I never did anything like that before, and the pickle juice is the only thing I can think of that might have caused it. It would also explain why someone would hide it away."

"Do your parents know about this?" asked Sammy.

"Actually, they don't. I sorta wanted to keep it a secret for now. I'm sure I'll tell them eventually."

"Ok, but I think you should soon. Maybe the people that made it are gonna want it back. Maybe you should just tell the police about it!"

"Maybe. I don't know, guys," answered Danny. "Let me go home and take another look around down there. Maybe I can find out more about this juice. In the meantime, Absolute Secret. Not a word of this to anyone on pain of death!"

Absolute Secret was the highest level of secret for Danny and his friends. Information on this level was never to be told over even under the most horrible tortures.

"Absolute Secret!" answered his friends.

"Should we come home with you? You know, help check this stuff out?" asked Joe.

"I think I'd better do some more searching on my own first," replied Danny. "Don't worry. I'll fill you in on anything I discover."

Joe raised his eyebrows, turned to Sammy and shrugged his shoulders. "Ok," he said. "No problem. Just keep us in the loop. And be careful!"

Joe and Sammy went on their way, and Danny watched them for a few moments. They were his best friends, but for some reason he wanted to keep this thing to himself, at least for a little while longer. He turned and started down the block to his new house, his mind still in turmoil. He remembered his first impression of the clutter in his basement, and the more he thought about it now, the more it seemed to him that the mess had been made by someone ripping apart the room while looking for something. Sammy was worried that the maker of the pickle juice might want it back. Danny thought that the people from whom it had been hidden, and who had been had been trying to find it, were the ones to be more concerned about. Regardless, he needed more information. Maybe if he poked around in the barrel room a bit more…

It was not really the driver's fault. He was just trying to make the light. Maybe he had sped up a little when the light turned yellow (as all New Yorkers know you are supposed to do). But the kid just stepped out into the middle of the street, right in front of him! He slammed on the brakes as hard as he could, but there was no way he was going to be able to avoid hitting the boy.

Danny heard the squeal of the brakes and glanced up to see a car hurtling toward him, only inches away. A moment of pure panic washed over him. There was no time to get out of the way. Without even thinking why, he closed his eyes and jumped.

He heard the car come screeching to a halt. The sound seemed to come from below him. Far below him. Strange. And he was holding on to something…? Danny opened his eyes to find himself gripping what looked like the branch of a tree. It wasn't one of the thicker branches that grow near the bottom. It was one of those thin, bendy treetop ones.

Danny looked down and almost threw up. He was hanging with both hands from one of the topmost branches of a tree, about fifty feet above the ground. The branch was bent almost in half from his weight. He tightened his grip on the branch, his heart beating rapidly. Down below, the driver of the car had gotten out and was looking around, scratching his head. He even bent down and looked underneath the vehicle. After some time (and impatient honking from drivers behind him), he shook his head confusedly, got back in the car and drove off.

Unexpectedly, Danny jerked several feet downward. The thin branch he was holding onto so tightly was beginning to peel right off the tree! He watched helplessly as the last connecting strands of bark began to rip away. There was nothing to do except squeeze his eyes shut and hope he wouldn't fall.

Even after all that had happened that day, he was still surprised when, in fact, he did not fall.

Danny was still holding onto the branch, which was now completely detached from the tree. He looked down again. He was not standing on anything. Why wasn't he falling? He gingerly stuck one toe down, but there was just empty air there. Then he took a full step. It was incredible – he was able to move around as though he was still on the ground! Just then, a gray New York City pigeon flew by, looking at him curiously. Danny watched the bird for a second, let go of the branch, then put out his arms like wings and willed himself in the bird's direction. It worked!

Danny laughed out loud with delight and propelled himself around the treetop a few times. This was the absolute greatest! Just wait until Joe and Sammy heard about this one!

The sound of the tree branch crashing to the street was loud enough to draw people's attention, and then to naturally look up to see where it came from.

"Hey, what is that up there?"

"Looks like a bird."

"Naw, it's too big. A small plane, maybe?"

"Wait, it…it looks like a kid!"

"Why would a kid be up there?"

"Hey, maybe they're making a movie or something!"

Some of the louder comments floated up to Danny, who was struck by the realization that flying around in plain sight might not be such a good idea. He quickly scooted back to the tree and began to climb down. Danny tried as much as possible to keep the tree trunk between him and the people that were still staring up into the sky. By the time he got to the bottom, most of them were already moving on. It takes something really extraordinary to hold a New Yorker's attention for more than a few seconds.

Unnoticed by Danny, the pigeon he had met at the top of the tree did not move on. In fact, it remained focused on the boy as he crossed the street and went into his house. Then the bird flew off into the distance, seemingly in a great hurry.

Danny let himself in and headed straight for the basement. He knew that Miri had a play-date with a friend, whose mother had arranged to pick her up from school. He had almost an hour alone before his mother got home from her job as a speech therapist, and he was determined to find out all he could. Any information as to what this juice actually was, how it worked, and what else it could do would be very useful, but Danny was really hoping to get some kind of clue as to who made it and hid it away. And why. He tapped out the pattern on the wall, jumped over the secret door as it descended and raced down the dark hallway with his pocket flashlight. As he ran, he thought again about all the trouble somebody went to in hiding the pickle juice, and a chill ran down his spine. Maybe whoever had torn up this basement looking for it was still out there. Maybe still looking, too! Danny definitely did not ever want to meet that person.

Danny descended the stairs to the pickle juice room and began wandering around and between the barrels. He was not sure what he was looking for, but anything that could give him some answers would sure be nice. He scanned back and forth along the floor as he moved through the underground chamber. Danny had made it all the way down to the end of the room when, in a corner behind the last row of barrels, he finally spotted something. Rushing over, he saw that it was a small flat metal box, closed with a simple clasp. Eagerly, Danny got down on his hands and knees and picked up the box. It was not that heavy. He shook it gently. A muffled thump came from within. Could all the answers be in here? Briefly, Danny thought about stopping his adventure for a little while at this point and bringing his parents into the picture. However, as when he first discovered the secret passage, he just could not wait.

Danny set the box down and tugged at the clasp. There was a brief hiss of escaping air, and then the box slowly opened.

The inside of the box was lined with a soft cloth interior of a deep red hue. Danny, squinting in the dim greenish light of the room, made out two objects nestled within. One was a bottle filled with some kind of fluid. The other was a rather plain-looking notebook.

Danny gingerly picked up the bottle. It was made of glass and filled with a dark, almost black liquid. He turned it around in his hands and almost dropped it when he saw what was on the other side. In the silence and dim lighting of the basement, the large white skull and crossbones that grinned up at him from the bottle unnerved him. He quickly put it back in the box, skull side down. Whatever was in that bottle was clearly meant to be off limits. A little on edge now, Danny stood up, glanced around the room a few times, then settled back down to the mysterious box.

Danny reached inside and carefully lifted out the notebook. It was a lined composition notebook, very much like the one Danny had used that same day in school. He turned it over a few times, understanding how important this book might be. It could be the only source of information about the mysterious pickle juice. The only place he might be able to find some answers to all of his questions.

There was no name or any other markings on the front or back. Danny considered the notebook for a few more seconds, then took a deep breath and opened the front cover.

The composition paper, crispy and yellowed with age, felt brittle in his hands. The first page of the notebook had a drawing of a human head in the upper left corner. The skin and bone of the top of the head was missing, so that you could see the exposed brain inside. The rest of the page was filled with what looked like extremely difficult math, with some arrows pointing to the brain. Danny turned some more pages, and all he saw were rows and rows of mathematical symbols and formulas. He supposed that it might be the formula or recipe for the pickle juice, but he obviously could not understand any of it. Danny flipped through the rest of the book, getting more and more frustrated as he went along. He had come down to the basement looking for answers, and all he had found were more mysteries. The math looked so complicated that he doubted that even Mr. Brown could figure it out. Then, on the bottom line of the last page of the notebook, he spotted something that he could understand, or at least he thought he did.

1 oz. = 1 hr

"Hmmm," muttered Danny. "I wonder…"

He peeked at his watch. It was about an hour and fifteen minutes since he had taken his first real drink of pickle juice, and he had swallowed maybe half a mouthful before he and his friends had bumped into BlackJack. The unique clear-headedness and strange tingling sensation that he had been feeling earlier seemed to have faded away. Was there a time limit on this stuff?

Danny picked up a loose piece of wood that was propped against the nearby wall and tried to break it in half. The only result was a nice long splinter in the palm of his hand. Danny winced in pain as the board clattered to the ground. Well, that settled it. At least one thing was clear now. One ounce of the pickle juice was equal to one hour of special abilities.

Danny turned back to the first page again and examined the picture of the open head. The formulas and equations sure seemed to have something to do with the brain. If the book explained how the juice was made and how it worked, that would mean…

It worked on his brain! It all made sense…each time BlackJack tried to hit him with something, he had concentrated on not being harmed, and nothing had hurt him! He had been able to fly because he had not wanted to fall down! This was incredible. The pickle juice seemed to have the ability to boost his brain function to the point that he could perform feats that were normally impossible! He remembered hearing stories about people who, in emergency situations, were able move heavy objects to save themselves or people they cared about, even though there was no way they could have done so under regular circumstances. Maybe this worked the same way.

Danny closed the book and put it back in the box. He grasped the top of the nearest barrel and put one foot on the faucet, then hoisted himself up so that he could get a good view of the whole room. The weird greenish light that filled the room was brighter in the area right above the tops of the barrels, almost as if it was emanating from the juice itself. Maybe it was. This had to be really powerful stuff, and there appeared to be plenty of it for him to use. All the same, the total amount *was* limited. He could have some fun for a while, maybe even for several years if he was careful, but eventually there would be no more pickle juice left. Even though the one he fell into the other day had been filled all the way to the top, maybe some of the other barrels were not. Maybe some were even empty! He would have to get around to checking each barrel to see how much he really had. Until then he would have to make sure not to waste any. He definitely wanted to enjoy this as long as possible.

Danny began making a mental list of all the awesome ways he could use the pickle juice. Forgotten for the moment were his concerns about the owner of the secret formula and those who had been trying to find it.

The faint sound of a car honk interrupted his thoughts. Danny glanced down at his watch and saw that he had been down in the basement longer than he had thought. His mother had come home! Fortunately, she always honked the horn as she pulled into the driveway, as if to announce her arrival. Danny hurried back to the regular basement and closed the secret door just as his mother walked in upstairs.

"Hi, Danny! Danny? Can you give me some help here?"

"Coming, Mom," said Danny, bounding up the stairs.

Danny helped his mother unload her speech therapy materials from the car. Mrs. Green would schlep big fabric bags full of toys and games all over Brooklyn so that the kids she gave therapy to would have some fun while she helped them improve their speech. Danny needed both hands to lift some of the bigger bags, and it crossed his mind that a small sip of pickle juice would make this job a lot easier. He did not know how his mother did it all day long.

When Danny had finished, his mother had one more chore for him. "Danny, do you remember Marty's Grocery? You know, we're just around the corner from there. Could you go and pick up some milk and orange juice for me?"

"Marty's? You're kidding! We're right around the corner from Marty's?"

"That's right. It's right on Avenue M, between 13th and 14th. I'm surprised you didn't recognize the neighborhood. But you were pretty small when we used to go there, I guess."

Marty's Grocery. Wow. That brought back some nice memories.

When Danny was younger, his parents took him to visit his uncle and aunt almost every week, and as a treat, they often stopped off at Marty's to say hello. Marty was a good friend of Mr. Green's family, and he always gave Danny a friendly welcome. Most of the time Danny also got a free delicious freshly - baked cookie, too. The Linzer tarts and rainbow cakes were Danny's favorite, and his mouth began to water as he remembered those days. He had not been back to Marty's since his aunt and uncle moved to Florida five years ago.

Danny got some money from his mother and headed out. His thoughts returned to the amazing events of the day. He had a basement full of stuff that allowed him to do things that people only dreamed about. To fly! Not to be hurt by baseball bats, and even knives! Imagine all the fun he could have! Who knew what other things the pickle juice would do? Even though there was that "one ounce = one hour" problem, and there wasn't an endless supply of the stuff, maybe it was not such a big deal after all. Why would he ever need to drink more than one or two ounces at a time? And even if most of the barrels were full or even half full, there should be more than enough to have fun for years and years.

Danny turned the corner and headed up Avenue M. There was Marty's, just as he remembered it. He wondered if Mr. Marty would remember him. He hoped that he wasn't too old to get some free rainbow cake.

The door jingled softly when Danny opened the door. A large, jolly looking man with bushy gray hair (grayer than Danny recalled) was standing behind a long counter to the right of the door. The man was wearing a long white apron. His eyes lit up in recognition as he noticed Danny.

"Well, if it isn't little Danny Green!" bellowed Mr. Marty. "Aha! But you are not so little anymore! I heard your family was moving here. Welcome to the neighborhood!"

There was a younger man standing next to Mr. Marty, also wearing an apron. He gave Danny a quick tight smile, then turned to Mr. Marty and said in a low voice,

"Dad, we really have to talk about this stuff. This problem isn't going to go away, you know."

"Fine, fine. We'll talk about it. But first we must welcome our young guest properly. Now, let me see..." Mr. Marty bent down below the counter, where all sorts of cookies and cake were displayed behind glass. "Rainbow cakes, right? And Linzer tarts!"

"How did you remember? That's amazing!" exclaimed Danny.

Mr. Marty chuckled. "When you run a store as long as I have, you learn how important it is to know your customer." He took two of each pastry and put it in a plastic wrap. "Here you go. On the house!"

"Thanks a ton, Mr. Marty!"

"My pleasure, Danny. You enjoy. You enjoy!"

Danny dug out one of the tarts and munched on it as he went down the aisle to the back of the store to get the milk and juice. Behind him, the good cheer and smile on Mr. Marty's round face was replaced with a troubled frown as he turned back to his son.

“Those men are going to be here soon, Junior. I guess we’d better count out the money for them.”

“We can’t keep on handing over all our hard work to those punks, Dad!” whispered Marty Jr. angrily. “We’ve got to stand up to them. Besides, the way things are going, I don’t know how much longer we can continue to keep the store open. They are taking too much from us!”

“Those ganiffs!” muttered Marty. “So, what should we do? Should we go tell the police, you think?”

“No, I don’t think that will work. I think we should just…”

Marty Jr. fell silent as the door jingled again, and two men in fashionable leather jackets, with dark hair and darker sunglasses, strolled in.

“Hey, Pops! How’s it goin’?” said the taller of the two, as he sauntered over to the counter. The shorter one plucked a two-liter diet cola from a plastic case nearby and starting drinking, straight from the bottle.

Without a word, Mr. Marty opened the register, took out a roll of bills, and started counting them out. His son looked on, getting angrier by the second. Finally, he could no longer hold himself back.

“Why don’t you just leave us alone already, huh?” blurted Marty Jr. “Haven’t you taken enough from us already?”

The shorter man lowered the bottle of soda from his lips and scowled. “Sounds like Junior here don’t appreciate our services, Frankie. Why don't we show him what happens when he's not under our protection?"

Frankie grinned wickedly. "My pleasure, Little John," he said, reaching into his jacket pocket.

"No, no, please, I'll pay you the money!" said Mr. Marty, shoving a fistful of bills at Frankie. "My son, he got a little excited. Please, just take the money!"

"I don't know, Pops," said Little John. "I think maybe we should teach Junior not to get excited so easily. It's very important to learn to control your temper. Not good for the health. Whadda you think, Frankie?"

Frankie grinned again and pulled a small black pistol out of his jacket. Mr. Marty turned white. Some of the money fell from his trembling hands. Marty Jr. raised his hands in the air.

Danny came walking up the aisle, wiping the last of the cookie crumbs from his face with his arm as he juggled the milk and juice. He was checking the containers for prices as he made his way to the counter, and was unaware of what was happening in the front of the store.

"Mr. Marty, how much is the...the...uh...uh…uh-oh…" Danny's voice trailed off as he took in the scene in front of him.

"You might want to go to the back of the store right now, kiddo," said Little John. "We got some business to discuss with Marty here. We'll be done real soon."

Frankie turned towards Danny, still grinning. His gun was pointed in the general direction of Marty and Marty Jr.

On any other day in Danny's life before this one, Danny

would have acted the way most people would have. He would have run to the back, found a corner to hide in, and hoped the bad men would go away without hurting him. But not today.

Instead of being scared, Danny got angry. Angry seeing weaker people being picked on by bullies, just like Shia and his friends picked on all the kids at school, and BlackJack and his gang had harassed anybody who went through "their" turf. And now Danny could do something about it. All he had to do was reach into his pocket and…

Where was that bottle? He was sure he had stuffed it into his pants pocket before he left. Or maybe he didn't. With a sinking feeling, Danny realized his pickle juice was probably still in his school backpack.

With both Frankie and Little John distracted by Danny's unexpected appearance, Marty Jr. saw his chance. He reached behind the counter and grabbed a baseball bat. He picked it up over his head and began to swing.

Frankie saw the movement out of the corner of his eye. He turned back toward Marty Jr. just as the bat came down on his gun hand.

The BANG! that followed was one of the loudest sounds that Danny had ever heard.

The money that had been in Mr. Marty's hand poofed into the air and floated to the floor. A red blotch appeared on his shirt. Mr. Marty gave a small gasp and crumpled to the floor behind the counter.

"Oh, no, no, NO!" yelled Little John. "This was not supposed to happen! Frankie, you idiot! What are you doing?!"

"Hey, boss, I thought the safety was on! Really, Little John! You've gotta believe me!" Frankie looked scared. He turned to Marty Jr., who was bent over his father, tears streaming down his face. "Look, Junior. I never meant to shoot your old man. But you shouldn't have swung that bat at me. Yeah, that's right. It's your fault!"

Marty Jr. stood up, his face a frightening mixture of anger and grief. He picked up the handset of the store telephone mounted on the wall behind the counter. The storekeeper's son looked at both men and said, in a strangely quiet voice, "GET…OUT…OF…OUR…STORE. NOW." Then he punched the numbers 9-1-1 into the phone.

"Come on, Frankie," said Little John. "We'll come back a different time. Cops'll be here soon. It's best if we're not around when that happens."

As soon as they had left, Danny rushed to the counter. "Is Mr. Marty OK? Is he going to be all right?"

Marty Jr. held up the palm of his hand to him as he began to speak into the phone. "My father's been shot. I'm at Marty's Grocery on Avenue M. Please get someone here right away!!" As Marty Jr. answered the emergency worker's questions, Danny looked around for some way to help. He gathered up all the money lying around on the floor into a neat pile and put it on the counter. He could already hear sirens in the distance as Marty Jr. hung up the phone.

Marty Jr. bent over his father again. With tears in his eyes, he whispered, "Dad, I'm sorry…I just couldn't take it that they keep stealing from us…Please…"

A New York Fire Department ambulance arrived, sirens blazing, shortly thereafter, followed closely by two NYPD patrol cars. The EMTs (Emergency Medical Technicians) hustled into the store and began to work on Mr. Marty. After a few minutes, one of them said, "Well, we've stabilized him for now. Let's get him into the ambulance." He turned to Marty Jr. "Your father was hit in the shoulder. We've got to get him to the hospital as quickly as possible. Come with us if you want to. The police can talk to you there."

"Of c-course. Let me just close up here."

A police officer entered the store at that moment. "No need, sir. We'll keep a man at the crime scene until you return. Go with your father."

Marty Jr. had gone very pale, and his hands were shaking as he locked the cash register. "Kid, you better go on home," he said to Danny. "You can pay me for your stuff some other time." Within a few minutes, the store was closed up and Marty Jr. was on the way to the hospital with the ambulance.

Danny walked home, shaken up by what he had just witnessed. Someone had gotten shot right before his eyes! Mr. Marty, who seemed like the nicest guy in the world! It just wasn't right! He wished with all his might that he had brought his pickle juice with him. But, could he have stopped those crooks? What if they had tried to shoot him? A knife from Blackjack was one thing, but would the pickle juice save him from a bullet? On the other hand, maybe they would not have been expecting a little kid to do anything, and he might have been able to surprise them…

His mother met him halfway down the block. She crushed Danny to her, crying. "Danny! Danny! Oh, I'm so glad you're all right! I heard all the sirens, and then I saw the ambulance going towards Marty's, and I was so worried!"

"I'm fine, Mom. But Mr. Marty got shot."

Mrs. Green's eyes widened. "Shot? You mean with a gun?"

"Uh-huh. But the ambulance guys said he'll probably be OK. Mom, let's go home, please?"

It took a while for Danny to fall asleep that night. An awful lot had happened to him that day, and all of it kept running through his mind as he lay in bed, especially the incident at Marty's. His parents had made him repeat it at least twice over supper, with his mother growing more nervous with each retelling. Miri sat through his story with her mouth wide open, looking terrified. Danny, though, got angrier each time he thought about it. How he wished he had taken his pickle juice! Surely he could have stopped those horrible people from almost killing Mr. Marty! Over and over, he imagined how he would have taken down those two bad men, just as he had done to Blackjack…

And then he was bouncing a ball off the front stoop of his house. Frankie and Little John had been sent to jail months before, after he had stopped them from robbing Mr. Marty's store. Everyone thought Danny was really brave and wonderful, and all the kids in his neighborhood wanted to be his friend. Even Shia and his gang thought he was too cool to start up with.

A man came walking up the street towards his house. There was something familiar about him.

"Hey, Danny. Remember me?" the man said, grinning cruelly.

"Hey, you're that guy from the store! Little John! I thought you were in jail!"

"I was – but I got out. And now I'm gonna get you back for putting me there." Little John pulled out a gun from his jacket pocket.

"I'm not afraid of you. That gun can't hurt me." Danny just sort of knew this was true.

"Oh, I'm not gonna shoot you, kiddo…"

Just then, the front door to Danny's house opened, and Danny's mother poked her head outside. Little Miri skipped out the door and down the stairs.

Little John laughed and raised his gun. "You'll learn the hard way not to mess with me and my boys, Danny. Sorry about your family, though! Hah!"

"NO! NO! STOP! DON'T DO IT!" screamed Danny. "LEAVE THEM ALONE!"

"STOP!!"

"STOP!!"

"Danny! Wake up! Danny! It's just a dream! Come on, son!" Danny's father was holding him tightly. "Whoa. That must have been some nightmare, Danny. Just calm down. Everything's fine. Shhhh…"

Danny trembled violently in his father's arms. It had seemed so real! He could still feel the panic of watching his mother and sister being placed into great danger – maybe even being killed! - because of him.

"What did you dream about, Danny? It might help if you told me about it."

"S-something bad was going to happen! I couldn't stop it!"

"It's ok, Danny. Shhhh. Just a dream."

His father stayed with him until Danny seemed to relax somewhat, then hugged him and went back to bed. But Danny did not feel relaxed. The dream scared him badly. The most worrisome part about it was that it *could* have been real. If he had actually stopped Frankie and Little John at Marty's store, what was going to stop them from taking revenge on his family? Or his friends? He really wanted to use his pickle juice to stop these kinds of people, but he would have to figure out a way to do it without anybody knowing who was doing the stopping.

"OK, Tommy, that's all for tonight. You've got school tomorrow – can't keep you up too late."

"Wait! You can't stop now! It's only…oh, it's 9:30. Already?" said Tommy, looking at his bedside alarm clock. "But hold on. How is he going to be able to do anything with the pickle juice if no one can find out? Is he going to wear a mask or something?"

"Not really. Those just wouldn't work in real life. You'll find out next time I visit. But you know the deal – if you're not asleep when your parents get back, they'll probably get a different sitter next time."

"Wait, wait. What do you mean, in real life? This is a true story? No way!!"

"Well, of course it's not exactly…well, why don't we talk about this next time. I really shouldn't keep you up any longer." Uncle Dan moved to the door. "Good night, Tommy. All your questions will be answered – in time."

CHAPTER 3

DANNY GOES FORTH

Later that week, as Tommy was having supper with his parents, his father cleared his throat and said,

"Tommy, your mother and I have a favor to ask of you."

"What is it, Dad?"

"Well, before you were born, your mother and I used to go out at night, sometimes to Manhattan to see a show, sometimes to a ballgame – just to relax and have some fun. Well, aside from a few nights ago, we really haven't had many chances to do that sort of thing, partly because we could not find a good babysitter. But you're older now, and Uncle Dan doesn't seem to mind, so…," Tommy's father glanced across the table at his wife.

Tommy's mother leaned across the table and held Tommy's hands. "Tommy, would you mind if Uncle Dan came over to watch you, say, about once a week?"

His parents were expecting some complaining, maybe even a small tantrum, but Tommy just smiled and said, "Sure! You guys have fun. Are you going tonight? Tonight's okay, I mean, if you want to."

The grownups looked at each other. Tommy's father

raised his eyebrows and said, “No, we’ll usually go out Saturday or Sunday nights. I’m glad you’re grown up enough not to mind being left with a sitter. Uh, thanks!” he added, patting Tommy on the back.

“That was a little too easy,” remarked Tommy’s mother, as Tommy went up to his room.

“I guess he gets along pretty well with Dan,” his father replied. “Dan was always good with kids, you know.”

That Saturday night, Tommy’s parents went out. Uncle Dan arrived, right on schedule, to watch Tommy.

“I heard we have a regular weekly appointment now, Tommy,” said Uncle Dan, as Tommy got into bed. “That’s good, because we have quite a ways to go yet. Are you ready?”

“Sure, Uncle Dan. You know, you still didn’t tell me where the pickle juice came from.”

“Well, our friend Danny doesn’t know either. Don’t worry, Tommy. Everything will be explained, but things must be done in the proper order. Now, let’s get to the story.”

Tommy settled back in his bed, and Uncle Dan resumed his tale.

The prisoner sat on his stone bench and sprinkled crumbs on the ground. Pigeons fluttered about, several landing on the bench next to him. One of them came to rest in his lap. He knew by the way that it was moving its eyes that there was something to report, but he could not allow the guards to notice any excitement on his part. Not that there was necessarily anything to get excited about. There had been several instances over the years when the bird had noticed something promising and had dutifully recorded it, but none of those occurrences had amounted to anything. Still, one could never give up hope. It was the only thing that sustained him in his dreary surroundings.

He checked the guards, who were ignoring him as usual. Cradling the bird in his hands, the prisoner gently tapped its chest twice. The pigeon's left wing flapped open and turned downward so that its underside faced the prisoner, revealing a small and extremely thin viewscreen. After one more glance back at the guards, the prisoner tapped the screen, which blinked on.

A boy's face appeared in the screen. A normal, regular face. There did not seem to be anything remarkable here, and the all-too-familiar feeling of disappointment began to settle in. Then the view expanded, and he saw the tree branches in the background. He let out a small gasp of excitement as he watched the boy first fall, then stop himself, and then incredibly begin to fly! He quickly tapped the screen again, making it wink off, and folded the bird's wing back to its natural position. He had to force himself to breathe normally and act as if nothing of importance had happened. The prisoner desperately wanted to watch the entire recording, but he was concerned that the guards would notice the attention he was paying to the bird. He would have to wait until tomorrow's outdoor exercise for further viewing. In the meantime, he would consider what he had already witnessed and mull over the implications.

The prisoner set the bird down on the bench next to him and whispered, "Go, my friend. Continue to observe the boy. He may be the one we have been waiting for."

That morning, Danny Green woke up early and got dressed quickly. He didn't feel tired, even though he had not had a restful night. The incredible events of the previous day kept replaying in his head. If only he had brought his pickle juice to Marty's! He could not help but feel partly responsible for Mr. Marty getting hurt so badly.

That's what was bothering him – the fact that he actually could have done something. Well, he hadn't, but that did not mean he should just give up. The next time those guys tried to bother Mr. Marty, he would be ready. In fact, he should always carry a bottle of pickle juice with him so that….

It was as if a light bulb went on in his head. He had found this awesome juice in his basement that let him do amazing stuff. Now he knew what he would use it for. He would try, as much he could, to stop this kind of thing from happening. Not just on his block, or in his neighborhood. It could be anywhere in the world. Anywhere that there were bad people who were hurting others, or forcing people to do things that they didn't want to. Why was it always the nice people like Mr. Marty, and the kids in Shia Dekel's class, who had to suffer? Let the bad guys feel what it was like to be pushed around for a change! Yep, as soon as school was over he would get out there and…

But there was that problem from his dream. How could he do all of this if his family and friends would be put in danger? Maybe he could have a disguise, or a mask of some kind? Nah. Somebody would recognize him eventually, or the mask would fall off. Danny decided to give it some more thought during his walk to school. If he could not come up with a good idea on his own, maybe Sammy and Joe could help him figure something out.

Danny passed by the kitchen and noticed Miri sitting at the table eating her favorite breakfast, a bowl of Unicorn Princess cereal. He really was not in the mood to deal with Miri and what she might have seen in the basement, but considering the way she was staring at the cereal box, that was not going to be a problem right now. The Unicorn Princess was Miri's favorite TV show, which of course was way too girlish for Danny to admit that he knew anything about. In truth, it was not completely awful. His mother had made him watch it with Miri on occasion because she got scared sometimes, and although it was mostly about unicorns and princesses, there was a pretty cool prince in the story as well. Miri was in complete agreement with him on that. In fact, she was practically in love with the dashing and handsome Prince Caprico. It often took Miri half an hour to eat breakfast when a Unicorn Princess cereal box was on the table, even more when the box had the prince's picture on it, and today was a prince day. She completely ignored him as he grabbed an apple from the fridge to eat on the way to school.

Danny checked his reflection in the hallway closet mirror as he reached for his backpack. He did not think he was ugly, but he was definitely no Prince Caprico. One thing he had to admit about the Prince, though. No matter if he was fighting dragons or swimming through waterfalls, his perfect coif of light brown, slightly curly hair was always precisely in place. Danny sighed as he ran a hand through his own rather bland and unkempt mop. He supposed these actors had armies of people working to keep them looking their best, but even his pickle juice probably couldn't help him in that area. Oh well. There were worse things to worry about, as his father was fond of saying. He checked his backpack to make sure that the still mostly-full bottle of juice was still inside, and headed off.

All during his twenty-minute walk to school, Danny considered his problem. How could he go around helping people yet keep his identity a secret? The best solution he could come up with was to make sure that nobody took a picture of him, or to put his hands over his face if someone tried. He did not have very much confidence in this strategy, though. Hopefully, Joe and Sammy would have some better ideas.

Danny's friends were already in the schoolyard when he arrived. Sammy noticed him first and came running over excitedly. "Hey, Danny! What's up? Did you find out anything else about that juice you found?"

Danny glanced around to make sure no one was listening. Joe was strolling over to them, trying to be more in control of his curiosity than Sammy was.

"Yeah, well, I got a lot to talk to you guys about."

"So, what's going on?" asked Joe.

Danny told his friends everything that had happened since he last saw them, including the incident at Marty's, as well as his dream in which he had prevented Frankie and Little John from hurting Mr. Marty. "So, I want to use this pickle juice to stop this kind of thing from happening, but I don't want anyone to know that I'm the one that did it" Danny concluded. "I couldn't think of anything that makes sense. You guys have any ideas?"

Before Danny's friends could answer, a large hand slapped down on Sammy's back, sending his glasses flying. "Oops! Sorry about that!" bellowed Shia. "That's what I've been telling you – accidents like that won't happen if you pay up. You dorks got the money?"

Sammy reached into his pocket sheepishly and handed over a five dollar bill. Joe, his eyes burning with anger and shame, sullenly dug four ones and four quarters out of his pocket.

"How about you, shrimp?" Shia asked Danny. "Where's my moolah?"

"Uh, sorry, Shia. I don't have it." With all that had happened to him the day before, Danny had completely forgotten about Shia's insurance business.

Shia beamed. “Hey, Ox! Mike! We got ourselves some fun over here!”

The rest of the Big Three ambled over from across the yard where they had been harassing some other kids, and formed a circle with Shia around Danny. Shia motioned to Ox, who grabbed Danny by the shirt and lifted him several inches up in the air. “So, squirt,” Shia sneered. “When am I getting my money? We wouldn’t want anything to happen to you – by accident, of course. Heh, heh.” Ox released Danny roughly, who managed to land on his feet.

After the previous day’s events, the Big Three did not scare Danny at all – they were just annoying. It was comforting to know that if he wanted to, he could make Shia and his gang eat their socks. Briefly, Danny considered going for his pickle juice and doing just that. After what happened at Marty’s, though, he could not bring himself to use it on these worthless punks. Better to let the Three think they were in control than to let even one ounce of the juice go to waste.

Meekly, Danny shuffled his feet.

“Uh, sorry, guys. I had a lot going on at home yesterday. I’ll bring it in tomorrow.”

Shia smiled. It was more fun to terrify people and watch them grovel than to simply beat them up.

“Why sure. No problem. I’m a reasonable guy. You bring in the money tomorrow – but there’s a dollar late charge.”

“Wait a minute,” said Mike, scratching his head. “He only has to bring a dollar tomorrow? That don’t make sense!”

“No, you idiot. That’s six dollars,” said Joe disgustedly.

"You want to watch your mouth, kid," said Shia. "I remember you. You're Joe. Yeah, you had an attitude problem last time you were in my class. Make sure I don't have to teach you some respect. It could get painful." He turned to Danny. "Six dollars tomorrow. Forgetting again would be a very bad idea. Mike, Ox, let's go!"

The Big Three wandered off to victimize some other boys. Joe stared furiously after them. "Danny! Why didn't you wipe the floor with them like you did to BlackJack? Gimme a break!"

Danny exhaled. "Believe me, I want to see them go down as much as you do. But I don't know exactly how much of this stuff I have, and I decided how I want to use it. I want to help people deal with real problems, like poor Mr. Marty. I don't want to waste it on some sixth grade goons."

"You mean you're just gonna let them get away with all this?"

"It's just not that important," Danny replied.

Joe shook his head. "Ohhh-kay, Danny. Your choice. I really don't agree, though."

The bell rang, and everyone headed inside. Danny leaned close to Sammy and whispered,

"How about you? Don't you think what I said makes sense?"

Sammy rolled his eyes. "I think you're out of your freaking mind, Danny!"

The rest of the school day passed rather uneventfully, except for when some of the teachers loaded up the boys with homework and assignments after being easy on them the first day of school. It was obvious that sixth grade was going to be much more serious than fifth grade had been. Danny picked up his head at one point during a particularly intense history class and looked around the room. Everyone was hard at work except for Shia and his gang. The scared kid from the first day, Martin, was sitting right next to Shia and taking notes furiously. Later, during recess, Danny heard that Martin had paid a month's worth of protection up front, and that Shia had been so happy that he had allowed Martin to become the Big Three's "special assistant". This new arrangement was made clear later in the day when Martin approached Danny just as he was about to start walking home with his friends.

Martin peered through his thick glasses at a notepad he was holding, looked up at Danny and said, "Green, right? Uh, remember to bring the money tomorrow."

"What did you just say?" Danny asked incredulously. You're Martin, right? You almost got your glasses broken yesterday! I can't believe this. You - you're working for them???"

"Traitor!" exclaimed Sammy.

"Look, guys. I don't know about you, but I'd rather be doing this than getting beaten up every day." Martin shrugged. "Sorry. Nothing personal."

Martin drifted away to find the next kid on his list, as Danny and his friends glared at the back of his head. Joe turned to Danny, anger blazing in his voice. "You're still going to let them get away with this stuff, Danny?"

"Hmmm," Danny muttered.

❧❧❧❧

Joe and Sammy spent most of the walk home from school trying to convince Danny to use his pickle juice to take down the Big Three. They were especially adamant after they passed the formerly threatening abandoned apartment building. At the mere sight of the boys, the remnants of BlackJack's gang that were still hanging out there had scurried out of sight like frightened mice. Their argument was simple – why this gang and not the Big Three? Danny finally promised them that he would think about it, just to get them to stop bugging him. Yes, using a boy like Martin against the rest of the class was a new low for Shia, but there were worse things going on in the world, and Danny still felt strongly that he should save his juice for the real problems.

They were approaching the corner of Avenue M and East 13th Street when Danny got an idea. "Hey, guys? Let's go check out Marty's. You, know, where the shooting happened yesterday."

Danny half-expected it to be closed, but there was Marty Jr., standing behind the cookie counter. The boys tentatively entered the store, which was empty of customers.

Marty Jr. raised his eyes at the sound of the door chime. Danny had never seen a face so miserable in all of his life.

Fearful of the answer but needing to know, Danny asked,

"How's Mr. Marty? Is he...um...did he…?"

"Oh, you're that kid that was in the store yesterday," said Marty Jr. "Yeah, he'll be fine, thank heaven. My father lost a lot of blood, but the doctors are pretty certain he will be ok. He even told me he wants to come back to work next week!" The storekeeper lowered his voice slightly. "He won't be able to come back that fast, though. He'll be out for a while. I - I just hope I can keep the store open until he comes back."

"What do you mean?"

"Nothing. Nothing that a kid should have to worry about. So, uh, you guys need anything?"

"No, thanks. We just wanted to check on Mr. Marty. And, I think I still owe you for the stuff I bought yesterday."

Marty Jr. grunted. "Whatever. Don't worry about it."

Danny and his friends turned to leave, and Marty Jr. resumed his stance behind the counter, staring glumly into space.

The boys exited the store quietly. "Wow," Joe said. "That was intense." Sammy nodded wordlessly in agreement. Danny turned to face them and exclaimed, "So, you see what I mean? I can actually do something about this! I…"

"Yeah, yeah, and you don't think the Big Three are as important," broke in Joe. "I guess you're right, sort of."

"Well, thanks!" answered Danny. He was relieved that his friends somewhat agreed with his decision. "Ok, now how about my problem? How do I go around stopping the bad guys without them finding out who I am?"

"How about a mask?" offered Sammy. "You, know, the ones with the eyeholes, like we used to wear for Halloween?"

"Yeah, I thought about a mask, but you remember how they were always slipping off? That would be a major fail. I don't know. Any other ideas?"

"Maybe you should put a bag over your head," said Joe. "Then you could hide your beeeee-youtiful face!" Sammy burst out laughing, and Danny couldn't help but smile as well.

"Seriously, guys. Help me out here."

By this time, they were in front of Danny's house. Joe shrugged his shoulders. "I dunno. I'm drawing a blank right now. Let me think it over a little."

"Let's do this," chimed in Sammy. "Why don't we each make a list of ideas? Tomorrow, we can see what we came up with and choose the best one!"

"Sounds good!" said Danny. "Let's do that. See you guys in the morning! Remember – Absolute Secret!"

Danny dumped his backpack on the desk in his room, closed the door and took out the bottle of juice. He twirled it over in his hands a few times. So far, he had tried this stuff only once, and in the short time that the juice had affected him, he had discovered that for every ounce he drank, he became extra strong, was protected from being hurt and could fly. Who knew what other amazing things he would discover about the juice's abilities? The only way to do that was to drink some more. Besides, he had to practice the things he already knew he could do. Especially flying. He would have to get good at that to be able to catch the kind of people who shot Mr. Marty. As far as keeping his secret, well, he would just have to be very careful. He'd go out for a little while, practice, then come right back. He would have to make sure no one took a picture of him, that's all.

Danny was feeling a little nervous, but he had made up his mind, and he did not want to chicken out now. He sucked some juice from the bottle, and, as the tingling sensations shot up and down his spinal cord, he felt that incredible clearness in his brain that he had experienced the day before. The edges of the furniture in his room appeared to come to razor-thin points, with their shadows in sharp contrast to the rest of the floor. The changeover to this enhanced state was less disorienting this time around, and now all he felt was this amazing sense of power and purpose, as if he could do anything he put his mind to.

Danny pulled back the curtains from his bedroom window and lifted the bottom pane. He poked his head outside and looked around. There was no one in sight. After taking a deep breath, Danny floated himself out into the small backyard of his home.

He hovered several feet over the ground, still not quite believing that he could do this. Danny moved himself around a little, getting the hang of willing himself through the air. Ok, he thought, this isn't so bad. I did this all yesterday. Now it's time to see how far I can take it. Danny again glanced around furtively to see if anyone was watching, then launched himself skyward.

Since the earliest of days, man has dreamed of the ability to accomplish what Danny Green was now doing. There is no way to accurately describe the feeling of being able to soar through the air at will, but I will try my best to portray what was going through Danny's mind as he experienced it.

Danny's initial surge upward left him about two hundred feet above street level. The neighborhood was spread out below him, with the houses and cars looking like toys from a city playset. A little further out to his left, he could see the green rectangle of the Brooklyn College football field, with the Manhattan skyline off in the distance beyond. Whoa! Danny's stomach clenched as he panicked slightly. This was a little higher up than he wanted to be! He closed his eyes and exhaled. It's ok, Danny told himself. I can keep myself up here. I won't fall. Gradually he calmed himself down and the little fearful twinge in his stomach passed. He opened his eyes and tentatively let himself drop, but slowly, until the tops of the houses and apartment buildings were substantially closer. It made him feel more secure that he had something close by to land on, if he had to.

Ok, Danny thought. This is better. Now let's see what else I can do.

He extended his arms and willed himself forward. Immediately his body moved several feet ahead. He put some more effort into it, and he suddenly shot forward quite some distance. It seemed he could make himself move in any direction just by aiming himself there, just as naturally as walking or running. As he gradually learned how to control his movements and speed, a huge smile broke out on Danny's face. This was definitely the coolest thing that had ever happened to anyone, ever! He zipped a short distance back and forth a few times, then, with a loud shriek of delight, let loose and went hurtling over the rooftops, soaring over several city blocks in less than a second. Danny felt more alive than he had ever felt before. He soared over the skies of Brooklyn in a state of pure bliss, and was soon doing loops and somersaults through the air like the most experienced circus performer. Even after only a few minutes, the flying was as instinctive to him as if he had been doing it all his life. His stomach did not lurch even when he was diving downwards, even though he had never been fond of roller coasters.

Danny's flight did not go completely unnoticed. An elderly gentleman who had been bird watching on the roof of his apartment building fell out of his lounge chair when Danny appeared in his binoculars. A fifteen year-old girl waiting with her friends on a corner for the light to change absent-mindedly glanced at the sky, and, with her mouth wide open, pointed and screamed, which made her swallow her gum. Within half a second, the rest of the girls were doing the same (screaming, that is). But the one who was eventually given credit for introducing Danny to the world was the little boy who lost his balloon. With the help of Benjamin Bowman, rookie reporter for Big Apple One News, of course.

In truth, he was not even a rookie. Benjamin was a mere intern at the cable news station Big Apple One, and it was only his third day on the job. Two days earlier, he had been shown around the station's Brooklyn headquarters by Bob, a tired-looking man who had been with the station for ten years and drank boatloads of coffee. Bob had walked the newsroom floor with him, showing him around and introducing him to the station personnel. Most of the reporters and other staff had been nice enough to shake his hand and welcome him to the "zoo". However, most of the good feelings generated by his introductory tour evaporated upon his first meeting with Mr. Petersen.

Ever since Benjamin had received notice that he had been accepted as an intern at Big Apple One (the only one from his college journalism class!), he had been dreaming of the moment when he would meet his idol, the legendary broadcaster Mike Petersen. Mr. Petersen had built his reputation by calmly and professionally reporting the six o'clock Action News for over twenty years to the citizens of New York for a major television network, and had just recently taken over the news division for the smaller Big Apple One cable station. Benjamin had noticed the famous face with its thick mane of distinguished graying hair from across the newsroom, and could not wait to meet him in person. Mr. Petersen had been sitting in his large corner office behind a massive oak desk. There were two other people in the office as well.

"Bob, do you think you can introduce me to Mr. Petersen? It would really mean something if I could get to meet him!"

Bob rolled his eyes. "Son, I don't think that's such a good idea. He's a very busy man, you know."

"Good luck on talking to Petersen," chimed in a reporter who had earlier introduced himself as David. "He hasn't said two words to me since he got here six months ago!"

Benjamin had not been discouraged. Mr. Petersen seemed so warm and reassuring on screen. How could he be anything other than friendly and pleasant in person? Benjamin had simply marched himself over to the corner office and opened the glass door.

The office was a bit intimidating. The walls were covered with framed photographs of Mr. Petersen with all sorts of celebrities, even a few past Presidents of the United States. The surface of the huge, dark brown desk was highly polished, and was empty except for a green felt blotter, a phone, and some folders of important-looking documents neatly stacked in one corner. Benjamin suddenly could not find his voice. "Uh…Uh…" is all that came out, as the three men stared at him.

"I can't believe he just went in there," whispered David to Bob. Bob nodded and adjusted his tie.

After a few more uncomfortable seconds, Mr. Petersen spoke in his well-known gravelly voice. "Yes? What can I do for you, young man? Are you the new shoeshine boy?"

"Uh, no," exclaimed Benjamin, finally finding his voice. "Actually, I'm your newest reporter! And, um, it's great to finally meet you! And to work with you! I mean, I don't think I'd be *really* working with you, like on a story or something, because today's only my third day, and…" The words had come tumbling out of his mouth before he could stop them. The two men sitting in front of Mr. Petersen's desk, both of whom were wearing expensive looking dark blue suits, smirked as Benjamin trailed off into an uncomfortable silence. His ears now turning red, Benjamin shuffled forward and stuck out his hand. "Um, I'm Benjamin. Benjamin Bowman." None of the men offered a hand in return, and after a few seconds, Benjamin withdrew his own.

Mr. Petersen seemed to be enjoying Benjamin's discomfort. "Look, Benjamin. Or can I call you Benjy? Wastes less of my time," he grunted. "You think you're a reporter? You can't just roll out of bed and become a reporter. It takes time to train and develop your instincts before you can spot a good story and convey it properly." Mr. Petersen chuckled, and the two other men immediately echoed him. "Listen, Benjy. Why don't you run along and get us some coffee, and maybe in a few months I'll find some small project for you to work on."

"Yep. Gotta pay your dues, kid," snorted one of the other men.

Benjamin had done the smart thing and walked out of the office before he said something that would get him fired. He heard the men laughing uproariously as soon as the door closed behind him. They thought he was just some worthless kid. Well, he'd show them. He would take his own camcorder out on the street and find some meaningful and inspiring story to report on. Then they would be sorry they treated him like that. And they would never call him "Benjy" again. He really hated that.

Well, that had been two days ago, and Benjamin was still searching. He wanted to make a major impression with his first story, but all he had been able to uncover so far were cute and easy pieces, very similar to what was happening right in front of him at the moment. A little boy was in tears because he had let go of his brand-new red helium balloon for just one second, and said balloon was now vanishing into the sky. The poor kid's mother was doing her best to make him feel better, but the boy refused to be consoled, screaming his adorable little head off while pointing at the swiftly receding balloon. Benjamin remembered, all too well, this very same thing happening to him when he was a kid. It just wasn't right. Why couldn't they make those things so that this would not happen? He idly flicked on his camcorder to follow the dancing red sphere. Someone really should do something about this….

Danny had come to a stop about one hundred feet above the intersection of Coney Island Avenue and Avenue M to admire the view. It sure was cool to be looking down at the world this way. Imagine if his bratty sister could see him now! Even her favorite hero, Prince Caprico, could not do anything like this.

A nearby movement caught his eye. He turned and saw a red balloon, about thirty feet to his left, floating away to wherever balloons go to when they escape from their owners. Danny zipped over and grabbed the string. The words "Metropolitan Bank" were printed on the balloon. Metropolitan Bank! His father worked for that bank! But he worked in Manhattan. What was this doing in Brooklyn? Danny peered downward. A large "Grand Opening" sign stretched across the front of a massive grey building below, and Danny remembered his father mentioning that his company would be opening a branch in Brooklyn soon.

On a nearby street corner, a little boy was crying hysterically and pointing up in the direction the balloon had been floating. It was quite clear what had just happened. Here was his first chance to use the pickle juice to help someone! He just hoped no one would recognize him. Danny willed himself down, feet first, balloon in hand.

He landed right behind the boy. Nobody seemed to notice that he had just dropped out of the sky. "Hey, kid, is this yours?" Danny asked, extending the balloon.

The boy turned to Danny. The tears stopped at once, and he grabbed the balloon gratefully. His mother looked at Danny in astonishment. "How did you get that? I saw it fly away ...oh, you must have gotten another one from the bank. That's so nice of you!"

Danny was going to explain, but decided it was best to say nothing at this point. He smiled and turned to go, when an unpleasantly familiar sound rang out. Several times, in fact.

BANG! BANGBANG!

Two men ran out of the bank, their faces covered by ski masks. One was carrying three bulging gray bags; the other was firing a pistol in the direction of the bank's front door. Danny heard glass breaking, followed by screaming from inside the bank. Someone nearby yelled "Get down! He's got a gun!" The boy's mother immediately pushed her son to the ground and covered him with her body. Most of the people on the street ducked down to the ground as well. But not Danny. This was exactly the kind of thing he wanted to stop. He was not going to let this happen. These were the kind of people who shot Mr. Marty, and he would not allow this to continue. His face heating up with anger, Danny advanced purposefully towards the bank robbers.

The men ran toward a nondescript car parked in front of the bank. The one carrying the money yanked open the front passenger-side door and shouted to the man in the driver's seat. "Let's go! Move it! We got the cash! Cops will be here any minute!" He jumped into the front seat, while the gunman slid in the back, keeping his weapon trained on the entrance of the bank.

The getaway driver did not need any further encouragement, and jammed his foot on the accelerator. The engine roared to life, rear wheels spinning madly. But the car did not move.

The driver pumped the gas pedal again. The wheels screeched into motion, but the car remained where it was.

"Come on, man! What are you waiting for? You wanna go to jail?"

"I'm tryin'! The car's stuck or something! Hey, wait a minute!" What's that kid doing back there?"

The driver had noticed a boy in the rear view mirror standing right behind the car. Something was off. It seemed – nah, it couldn't be. He rubbed his eyes and squinted into the mirror again. The boy's hands were under the trunk, and he appeared to be lifting the back of the car off the ground!

"There's some kid holding up the car!"

"What?!? What are you talking about?"

"I'll take care of it!" muttered the driver, as he put the car in park and drew his own gun. He could already hear sirens in the distance, and he did not feel like spending the next few years in prison.

Danny was holding the rear end of the car off the ground with both hands, but it was so easy for him that he felt he could do it with one pinky. He would have to practice lifting heavier things when he got the chance. Maybe a cement truck? A nasty-looking thug, who was yelling and pointing a gun at him, broke his train of thought.

"I don't know how you're doing that, but drop the car, kid! Now!"

"NO!!' said Danny defiantly. "Only if you give back the money. I am not gonna let you rob that bank!"

By this time, many of the people who had been lying on the ground had cautiously begun to lift their heads, among them Benjamin Bowman. Benjamin had been following Danny on camera from the moment he had flown into his viewscreen. At first, he thought the whole thing was some kind of publicity stunt for that nearby bank's grand opening. He had assumed that they had gotten some circus kid to perform, with wires holding him up or some such trick. The more he followed Danny with his camera, though, the more he realized that, incredibly, this was legitimate. Not an act. He could not begin to comprehend how this was possible but he was determined to follow it through to the end, regardless. If this kid was the real thing, he was on to the story of the century.

Benjamin lay low behind a parked car but kept his camera trained on Danny. What did this kid think he was doing, standing up to these armed and dangerous men? And how in the world was he holding up that car? Forget that – how about the flying?

The getaway driver cocked his weapon. "Kid, I'm serious about this, and I don't have time to argue. DROP IT!!"

Danny was not at all sure that the pickle juice was powerful enough to protect him from the gunman. Blackjack and his knife were not quite in the same ballpark as a speeding bullet. He just did not think this guy would really shoot him. He was only a kid, after all.

As it would turn out, Danny was quite wrong about this.

"NO!" repeated Danny.

"Ok, kid, I gave you your chance. If that's the way it's gonna be…."

The driver began to pull the trigger.

Oh no, Danny thought. He's really going to shoot me! He panicked, dropped the car, and fell into a crouch, with his arms covering his face. Tears formed in his eyes as he braced for the bullets' impact. He never realized that trying to help people would lead to this. Perhaps he should have. It was not turning out to be as much fun as he thought.

Please, please. Don't...

The people in the crowd gasped as they witnessed the armed criminal fire at the defenseless boy at point-blank range. They winced as the gunman, not seeing any blood, continue to fire in a mindless rage until he emptied his weapon.

Danny heard the gun roar over and over, but did not feel anything. Maybe the shooter missed? But he was so close!

Danny lowered his arms slowly. There were shiny twisted pieces of metal lying on the street around him. He picked one up. It looked like a bullet, but one that had hit something so tough that the pointy end had split open and bent backward so that it was almost completely inside out. And, incredibly enough, it seemed that *he* was that tough something.

The driver did not know why the boy was not full of bullet holes, and at that point, he didn't care. The kid had dropped the car, and those sirens were getting closer. He jumped back into the front seat, threw the car into drive and mashed down on the gas pedal.

"Hey! They're getting away!" someone yelled. But almost everyone was still staring unbelievingly at Danny, who continued to turn the twisted bullet over in his hands. It was hard to wrap his mind around how powerful the pickle juice was turning out to be. He had not even felt a bullet!

Just as the getaway car reached the end of the street, two

police cruisers arrived to block its escape. The driver slammed on the brakes to avoid colliding with the NYPD vehicles. As the getaway car screeched to a halt, several police officers charged forward with their guns drawn.

"STEP OUT OF THE CAR WITH YOUR HANDS IN THE AIR! YOU ARE UNDER ARREST!"

The three men were surrounded, and had no choice but to give up. The officers quickly moved to take control of the criminals as they slowly exited their vehicle.

Everybody in the crowd, including Danny, clapped and cheered. But while Danny was cheering on the police officers, the rest of the crowd was actually directing their applause at Danny.

As the police handcuffed the bank robbers, one of the officers remarked to his partner, "Are these guys getting slower, or just dumber? That alarm went off ten minutes ago. Why are they still here? They should've been halfway across town by now!"

The getaway driver was being pushed into one of the patrol cars and overheard. "Well, we would've, if not for that freak kid!" he barked.

"What are you talking about? What kid?" shot back the police officer.

"That kid you got working for you! I shot him five times and he didn't even get scratched!"

The policeman's face darkened. "You shot a kid? Where?!" He glanced down the street and saw a crowd gathered around a boy in front of the bank. "I'm going to check on that," he told his partner. "Better call an ambulance. I can't believe this dirtbag shot a kid!"

The officer sprinted over to the boy, who seemed to be doing perfectly fine. Still, he had to make sure.

"Excuse me, son, my name is Officer Thompson. Is everything all right here? I heard there was a shooting."

"Yeah, he's all right!" yelled out someone from the crowd. "See that stuff on the floor? That's bullets, man! This kid is bullet proof!"

"That's right, officer!" shouted someone else. "You got to get more of these kids out there! He stopped those robbers cold!"

Officer Thompson bent down to pick up one of the twisted bullets, shifting his eyes between it and the boy in front of him.

Benjamin had been filming the whole time, although he was tempted more than once just to put down the camera and take in the amazing events like everyone else. If he wanted to become a professional newsperson, though, keeping focused on the story was what he had to do. To get the full picture, he needed more information. Who was this kid? How did he do these fantastic things? He had not even gotten a clear frontal shot of the kid's face yet. Now, during this brief pause in the excitement, he saw his chance.

Danny was starting to get a little uncomfortable from all the attention he was getting. The police officer was holding one of the bullets and staring at him, as was everyone else in the crowd. Then someone came forward holding a video camera, and Danny suddenly remembered that the last thing he wanted to happen was for anyone to find out who he was. Having a video taken of him would definitely not be helpful.

"Hi, uh, I'm Benjamin Bowman with Big Apple One News. Uh, can you tell us how you picked up that car? And how bullets can't hurt you?"

Danny's face turned red. "I – I'm sorry. I can't…I really just have to go." Danny turned around and began to walk away.

"No, wait! Who are you? What's your name?" Benjamin hurried after Danny, hoping to get some answers.

Danny turned around once more. He was met by the clicks of a dozen cell phone cameras. He quickly brought his hands up in front of his face, although he got the sinking feeling that it was far too late to prevent his picture from being spread around the world.

Officer Thompson stepped in between Danny and the cameras. "Okay, folks, let's give the kid some room, here. He….what, what's going on?" A startled gasp had erupted from the crowd, their eyes raised to the sky. The officer turned to see Danny rising up past the rooftop of the bank.

"Holy smokes!" muttered Thompson. He took off his cap and, along with everyone else, watched in utter amazement the awesome spectacle of a boy rising into the air under his own power.

Benjamin kept the camera on Danny until he was no longer visible. He could not believe his fortune. He had just witnessed, and recorded, an event of historic proportions. Experienced reporters could slog through their entire careers without getting a shot at this kind of story, and he had nailed it in his first week on the job. He could not wait until he got back to the newsroom and heard what Mr. Petersen had to say about this!

After Danny disappeared from view, Benjamin turned the camera on Officer Thompson. "So, Officer, any thoughts on our mystery kid? Any idea who he is or where he came from? And why," said Benjamin, sniffing the air thoughtfully, "did he smell like pickles? I just realized that."

Officer Thompson was still looking at the sky, where a single gray pigeon was circling over the area. "I have no idea," he replied dazedly. "But come to think of it, he did smell like pickles. Sour ones." Thompson shrugged. He realized that his job had just gotten a lot more interesting. And complicated. He turned to walk back to his squad car. "I just hope he stays on our side."

"Uh-oh. I guess his secret isn't going to last that long," broke in Tommy. "They'll show that video everywhere!"

Uncle Dan glanced at his watch. It was getting a little late, but he had some more time, and he did not want to leave Tommy hanging. Not at this particular point, anyway.

"Well, as I mentioned earlier, nothing in this story is that simple. Tell you what. I'll continue the story some more, but I am not going to have time for any questions later. Save them up, and I'll try to answer them the next time I come."

CHAPTER 4

TRIALS AND TROUBLES

Danny was furious with himself as he powered away from the scene of the robbery. How could he have been so stupid? His first time out, and he had not been careful enough to prevent his face from being seen. As soon as that video made it to the internet, his secret would be history! He was sure his parents would be less than thrilled when they found out what he had been up to. He would have to tell them about the secret room in the basement, and what he had found there. They would probably take away all of the pickle juice and give it to the police or the army. And when those bank robbers got out of jail and found out that Danny Green had been the one who put them there, well, it would most likely turn out just like his dream, and there would be nothing he could do to stop them.

He had not aimed himself in any particular direction on his flight away from the bank, and had not been paying attention to where he was going. Danny was surprised to discover that he was now flying over open water. A quick scan of his surroundings revealed that he was over the ocean, about three hundred feet offshore of Coney Island Beach. A Ferris wheel and the famous Cyclone Roller Coaster were visible straight ahead, just behind the wooden boardwalk. Danny could see that people on the beach and on the boardwalk were beginning to notice him, and, not wanting further attention, swooped down low near the surface of the ocean waves, startling the occupants of a nearby sailboat.

As he flew along, he kept on hearing a curious flapping sound. At first, he thought it was coming from the sails of the boat he had passed by, but the sound did not decrease in volume as he sped away. He twisted himself around, trying to find the source of the noise, and in the process discovered that the sound was coming from him. What was left of his shirt, to be exact. Although the pickle juice had made him bulletproof, it seemed that his clothing was not. His shirt and undershirt were spotted like a leopard's skin with black-ringed bullet holes, from which strips of cloth fluttered in the breeze.

Oh, that's just perfect, thought Danny. Even if, by some amazing stroke of fortune, no one recognized his picture, he would have to come up with some explanation for the shirt. Unbelievable. This pickle juice was definitely turning out to be more trouble than it was worth.

Danny put on a burst of speed and headed back to shore, increasing altitude again as he went. The day had certainly not gone the way he had anticipated, especially after all the promise the afternoon had started out with. At this point, all he wanted to do was dive under his covers and hope this was all a dream from which he could wake up. Maybe it was not so bad, though. Maybe they had not gotten a clear picture. As far as his ruined shirt was concerned, he could quickly change clothing when he got home, maybe toss it in the trash later, his mother might not notice…

What happened next could best be compared to the dimming of the lights that occurs during an electric power shortage, or perhaps the sputtering of a car engine that is almost out of fuel. First there was a flickering in his vision, from enhanced extra-clear to normal and back again. Then, without warning, Danny found himself falling out of the sky! He dropped uncontrollably about halfway to the pavement before he was frantically able to bring himself out of the dive. What in the world...? He looked at his watch. Nearly an hour had passed since he had taken the shot of pickle juice. He had not swallowed that much because he had not planned to be out that long, and apparently he was running out of power! He felt his pockets for the bottle, only to remember that it was still on his desk in his bedroom. Danny's heart began racing. This was just getting better and better, wasn't it?

Trying his best not to panic, Danny forced himself to get a grip on his thoughts. The most important step was to get to the ground as soon as possible. It would not be pleasant to be fifty feet up when he completely ran out of gas. He scanned the area below, a residential block of about forty houses, each with a small patch of green in front and a slightly larger yard in the back. One particular house was almost twice as large and much more extravagant than any of the nearby homes. It had a wide driveway that led from the street to a huge green backyard that was almost as big as a small park. Well, if he was going to crash, better on grass than on concrete. Danny aimed himself at the area behind the fancy house and hoped for the best.

He barely made it, as he felt the last of his ability to fly give out while he was still a few feet above the ground. Danny made an awkward belly flop into the turf, ripping his clothing further and muddying them up for good measure. Surprisingly, the impact did not hurt him, though it left a boy-sized ditch in the otherwise perfectly groomed grass. It seemed that whatever was left of the juice was still able to protect him, though he could sense that this, too, was draining away by the second. He really had to be getting home as soon as possible.

Danny got to his feet and was about to head down the driveway and toward the street, when an all-too-familiar-looking boy exited the side door of the mansion, right into his intended path. Two other kids followed close behind, bellowing loudly and off-key the theme song from some afternoon TV show they had just been watching. The first figure turned towards the backyard and spotted him, and immediately began advancing toward Danny menacingly.

"Hey, you! Creepo! What are you doing in my backyard?"

The other two-thirds of the Big Three fell silent and began to smile, cruelly, at the fate that awaited the kid with the tattered clothing who had trespassed on Shia Dekel's personal playground.

Benjamin ran almost the whole way back to the news station. He would have taken a cab, but the events of the afternoon had caused traffic to come to a standstill for almost a mile in each direction, as the police tried to get a handle on what had just happened. His dirty blond hair was matted with sweat and his shirt mostly untucked by the time he made it through the office door. He need not have worried about his unprofessional appearance, as the newsroom was in complete pandemonium. It was quite obvious what all the fuss was about. Reporters were talking excitedly into their phones,

("You saw WHAT?")

("A kid was shot? And he was dying? Flying? No, that can't possibly have…")

("He picked up a car? You have any independent confirmation on this?")

secretaries were running around with folders full of

papers, and Bob, appearing more exhausted than ever, was standing outside his cubicle surrounded by some of the more experienced staff, trying to make sense of the chaos. Not knowing who else to turn to, Benjamin headed in that direction.

"OK, people, Petersen's out of the office, and is unreachable. We have to decide how to action this story for tonight's news. What facts do we have so far?"

One reporter with graying black hair and wearing a pinstriped suit and blue silk tie spoke up. "Well, Bob, this is what we got. We have unconfirmed reports of a ten or eleven year old boy stopping a bank robbery by simply picking up the getaway car. The kid was then shot four or five times at point-blank range, and either all the bullets miraculously missed or even more incredibly, uh, I'm not sure how to say this…"

"Bounced off him!" piped in Benjamin, who was now standing on the fringes of the group. He was the youngest one there by about twenty years. The others turned to look at him in mild irritation.

"Who's this?" asked a thin red-haired female reporter.

Bob cracked a tired smile. "Everybody, this is Benjamin, our new intern. Some of you may have met him the other day…"

"Oh, you're the kid that got flattened in Petersen's office. Nice going, rookie," smirked the man with the blue tie, in a friendly sort of way.

"Go easy on him, Brian. He was trying to use some initiative. Something we need right around now." Bob paused and noisily blew out a mouthful of air as he held up some photos for all to see. "These are the best pictures we've been able to access, mostly off the internet." The reporters all crowed in closer to Bob. Benjamin was still on the outside of the group, and had to stand on tiptoes to be able to see anything. The clearest photo featured a reasonably good picture of the boy's face and upper body, with what looked like a bullet hole torn in his shirt. The rest were more hurried and blurred, and were mostly of the kid's back as he flew away. Not one of the pictures was of good quality, and all had obviously been taken by cell phone cameras.

"The other news stations are all scrambling for more information on this," continued Bob. "If we can somehow come up with something, perhaps some unique information…"

"What about a complete video of this kid appearing on the scene, including the whole robbery, shooting and all, plus the kid actually flying away at the end?" came a voice from the back of the crowd.

Everyone turned to look at Benjamin again. "I would give my left lung to have such a video," whispered the red-haired woman.

"Nothing's worth that much, Rachel, but that would be quite a scoop!" remarked Brian.

Benjamin took out his camcorder. "Can I plug this into someone's computer?"

"Sure. Use mine," said Bob.

Benjamin made his way through to Bob's desk, fished out a USB cable from his camera bag, and hooked up the camera to the computer. After a few seconds, the computer recognized the camera and some video icons popped up. He double-clicked on the correct file and the video, expanded to full-screen size, began to play.

A hush enveloped the small group of reporters as they

watched the roughly seven minute clip. As other office personnel realized that something was going on, more people joined the crowd around Bob's desk, until by the end of the video almost everyone in the newsroom was surrounding the area, trying to get a glimpse of Benjamin's footage. When it was over, Benjamin looked up at Bob, who seemed in a state of shock.

Rachel finally broke the silence. With more than a hint of jealousy, she demanded,

"How on earth did you get this?"

"I was just in the right place at the right time," answered Benjamin.

"You certainly were. You certainly were," repeated Bob absentmindedly. Then he snapped his fingers. "We have to get hold of Petersen. We can scoop every other station in the world if we get this out there for the six o'clock newscast. Where is that crusty old curmudgeon, anyway?"

David, a reporter Benjamin had met on his first day, spoke up. "Ask Dekel – he'll know! He's like, Petersen's right hand man!"

Bob detached Benjamin's camera from his computer, grabbed it and Benjamin, and, followed by most of the newsroom staff, headed towards Mr. Dekel's office, which was two offices down from Mr. Petersen and about half as impressive. Benjamin recognized him as one of the two men who had been in Mr. Petersen's office the day he had made a complete fool of himself. Mr. Dekel, a large and impressive man wearing an expensive grey pinstriped suit with gold cufflinks, waved Bob in after fixing the rest of the staff with an annoyed frown, which only grew more pronounced when Benjamin entered his office right behind Bob.

"Mr. Dekel, you've got to contact Petersen. Where is he?"

"If you must know, he's playing golf with the CEOs of several important corporations. He left strict instructions not to be disturbed unless there is a national emergency," replied Mr. Dekel in a haughty tone. "And I highly doubt anything you've turned up fits that description. I've seen nothing on the newswires to indicate any such event."

Bob turned to Benjamin. "Shut the door, kid. No, no, you stay in here," he said, motioning Benjamin over. Benjamin had assumed Bob wanted him to leave, and he had been about to do so. Bob turned back to Mr. Dekel and spoke with a controlled fury that Benjamin would recall with awe for the rest of his journalistic career. "We have a chance here to break one of the biggest stories of all time. It hasn't made the wires yet because it's local, and it happened less than half an hour ago. This young man," he pointed to Benjamin, "was fortunate enough to be there and catch the whole thing on tape. Even more fortunately, he works for us!" He offered Benjamin's camcorder to Mr. Dekel.

"Sir, you've got to step up and make a decision on this. You are the senior executive in the office right now. Help us get this on the six o'clock, and maybe next time Petersen will bring you on the golf trip and not that toady, Stevens!" exclaimed Bob, pointing towards the office in between Mr. Dekel's and Mr. Petersen's.

Mr. Dekel gulped audibly and took the camcorder, holding it like a hot potato. Bob waited a bit, then nodded to Benjamin, who gently retrieved the camera from the executive's trembling hands. He then used his USB cable and hooked it up to Mr. Dekel's computer. As the executive watched the clip, his mouth dropped open in disbelief. When it finally ended, he turned to Bob and whispered,

"This is for real? Not some trick computer special effects?"

"Everything we've been hearing on the street confirms what's on that tape. And it seems we're the only ones with this kind of footage."

"Who is this kid? Do we have any idea?"

Bob turned to Benjamin. "Did you catch anything on that, Benjamin?"

"Sorry. No idea. The kid started to get all upset when I started asking him about himself."

"Did you notice any particular characteristics? Funny voice? Bites his nails, maybe?"

"Well, there was that smell. I got a whiff of sour pickles after he jumped away. Must've been the updraft. The cop noticed it, too."

Mr. Dekel rubbed his eyes, regaining some of his composure. "So. Not much in the way of facts to go on here, gentlemen. Just that he smells like pickles. But that is one great piece of footage." He rose from his chair and paced back and forth behind his desk for a few moments before speaking. "You know, we go back a long way, Bob. I never understood why they gave this job to me instead of you. Maybe Petersen thought I would be more of a yes man. Lord knows, quick decision making is not for me." He paused a moment, then continued. "But if we don't get this on the air, we will lose the chance to give Big Apple One the lead on the most extraordinary story I have ever seen." He looked at his desk clock, which read 4:30 PM. "I'm making the call," said Mr. Dekel, and reached for the phone on his desk.

"Susan, get the boss on the phone. I think we have a major story on our hands!"

Bob flashed Benjamin a thumbs-up as they watched the executive nervously tap his fingers on his desk. After a minute or so, a woman's voice came through the speakerphone.

"Mr. Stevens says that Mr. Petersen is in the middle of his game and does not want to be disturbed unless the world is coming to an end. What should I tell him?"

Mr. Dekel looked up at Bob and Benjamin, then back at the phone. "Never mind, Susan. I'll deal with it from here." He moved his index finger to push another button on the phone, hesitated, took it away, then sighed, straightened himself, and jabbed it down decisively.

"Dekel here. Tell the broadcast division we have late breaking news for the six o'clock. Highest priority! I'll send over the material in a few minutes."

Benjamin could hardly contain his excitement. He had done it! The big time! His footage would be broadcast for all to see! He turned to Bob. "Thanks, sir! I really appreciate it! You too, of course, Mr. Dekel!"

Mr. Dekel addressed Benjamin. "It seems I underestimated you a few days ago. I forgot how I, too, was once a rookie reporter. In fact, if not for Bob, here, I probably never would have amounted to much at all. Good work, son." Mr. Dekel stood up to shake Benjamin's hand. Then as he sat back in his black leather chair, a frown crossed his face. "I just hope I still have a job tomorrow morning," he muttered. Benjamin raised an eyebrow to Bob, who did not respond.

Neither Benjamin Bowman nor Bob, and certainly not Mr. Dekel, considered that what might be a great success for Big

Apple One might not be such a positive experience for the mystery boy at the center of their history-making newscast.

Danny shielded his face with his right hand as if he were trying to block the sun from getting in his eyes. The Big Three did not seem to have recognized him as one of their classmates yet, and he would love to keep it that way.

The only way out of Shia's backyard was down the driveway. Unless he tried to jump over the fence…Nope. Too high. Danny didn't think he had enough juice left for that. And if he tried to climb, Shia would yank him down before he could get halfway up. Well, he could always try manners and common sense…

"Hey, listen – sorry about being in your yard. I'll leave right away, ok?"

Shia smiled pleasantly. "No problemo. Come back and visit anytime!"

"We have been pleased to make you an acquaint-enance!" said Ox with an exaggerated bow. Mike did not bother with the false pretensions; he just rolled up his sleeves and closed his fists. Danny, who had entertained a slim hope that Shia might actually let him go, caught this out of the corner of his eye and realized it was not to be. Still, perhaps if he ran for it….

The driveway was quite wide, and the Big Three were standing bunched in the middle of it. Danny made a sudden move and took off down the left side of the driveway like a football player racing down the sidelines towards the end zone. He still had some extra speed from the pickle juice, and he almost made it.

Shia had started moving as soon as Danny did, though, and was a lot quicker than he looked. As Danny went racing by, Shia shoved him really hard from behind. Danny lost his balance and went sprawling to the concrete. The very last of the juice's protection expired as he landed painfully on his hands and knees, scraping them rather badly. With tears in his eyes, and with the Big Three's scornful laughter ringing in his ears, Danny staggered to his feet, his scratched and bleeding palms an aching reminder of how quickly and dramatically his situation had changed in the last few minutes.

"Good one, Shia!" roared Mike. "Look at the little crybaby. Oh, I think you messed up his hair!"

"Yeah. Boo hoo hoo!" added Ox.

"You know, that was a pretty good move," Shia commented, turning away from the helpless Danny. "I've got to remember that one for school, to use on our favorite customers. That should remind them to pay up!"

Danny kept his face turned away from the Big Three and stumbled down the driveway.

"Hey! He's leaving!" blurted Ox. "Are we done with him already?"

"Yeah, let him go. I don't want to touch him more than I have to," answered Shia. "Did you see his clothes? I mean, come on…"

The pain in Danny's knees began to fade slightly as he reached the sidewalk and began his long walk home. He had a nice-sized hike ahead of him, and he didn't know if he was up to it. Danny was feeling pretty miserable, both physically and mentally. With his clothes in tatters and covered with bits of dirt and grass, he had the look of someone who had just been on the wrong end of a major beatdown.

Everything had gone wrong. Even the good stuff he had done was probably going to get his picture all over the news. The only bright side was that, by some miracle, Shia and his gang had not recognized him as one of their classmates. However, that was little consolation, since the cat would be out of the bag soon enough. Then, as Danny stumbled down the street, he was hit with the realization as to how truly devastating the revelation of his secret could potentially be.

He recalled what his basement had looked like before he started to clean it up. Like someone had overturned everything in it because they were determined to find something important. Something he now knew to be the pickle juice. Whoever had been searching for it could still be out there. If he, or they, realized what Danny had discovered, and worse, found out who he was and where he lived...Danny shuddered. He highly doubted that whoever had been trying to find the pickle juice all those years ago was going to turn out to be a friend of his. Quite the opposite, most probably.

Although he was usually one of the last, if not the last, employee to leave every day, Mr. Green liked his job as the chief accountant at the main offices of Metropolitan Bank, located a few blocks from Grand Central Station in Manhattan. Most bank employees were long gone by the stroke of 5:00 PM, but his demanding responsibilities meant that he rarely left before six fifteen. In fact, he usually ended up working past eight o'clock several times a month, just to ensure that his many tasks were completed. Nevertheless, the work was important and fulfilling. He helped determine exactly how profitable the bank was, where the bank should invest its extra cash, and what interest rates it should offer its customers. He reported directly to the Chief Financial Officer, a reasonable and knowledgeable fellow named

Mark Lowenstein, whom he got along with rather well.

It was therefore somewhat of a surprise when Mr. Lowenstein stuck his graying head into Mr. Green's office a few minutes before five o'clock and remarked,

"Hey, Jack. You might want to head on home early tonight. Like, now."

"Why? What's up?"

"It seems that that there was an attempted robbery at the new Brooklyn branch this afternoon."

"Oh my G-d!" Was anyone hurt?"

"No, no one was hurt, and that's very fortunate, but here's the amazing part. It seems that the robbery was stopped by some kid! The branch manager even has witnesses who claim that this kid was shot several times and walked away without a scratch! Actually, and this is really funny," Mr. Lowenstein chuckled, "there are those who insist that the boy flew away, into the sky. Flew away! Can you imagine that?"

"That's ridiculous!"

"Yeah, it's crazy. Anyway, the bank president is telling everyone to go home early, not to get stressed out over what happened. Also, Big Apple One has leaked that they have an exclusive video of the whole thing, which they are going to put on the six o'clock news. If you want to make it home in time, you'd probably want to leave now."

"Well, thanks, Mark, but maybe I'll just check the internet later. I've got to start work on the call report, you know…"

"Jack, the president of the bank is insisting that everyone

go home. Apparently, Big Apple One is claiming this is history-making stuff. Hey, don't you have a son about twelve years old? Danny, right? They say this kid was about the same age. Your boy would get a real kick out of seeing this. Go watch it with him!"

Intrigued, Mr. Green raised his eyebrows. "Sounds a little farfetched. But if the boss says go home, I'm outta here. I guess I'll just stay late tomorrow instead."

Mr. Green shut down his computer, packed up his briefcase and headed to the elevators. He hoped there would not be any delays on the subway, or he wouldn't make it home in time.

Thirty minutes later, a limping and exhausted Danny finally reached the corner of Avenue N and East 13th. His house was much closer to the Avenue M side of the block, about twenty houses down. He had not really gotten to know any of the neighbors yet, and Danny, very conscious of his ragged appearance, avoided them as much as possible by walking in the street rather than the sidewalk. He also tried to keep parked cars between himself and any passersby. Danny had never felt happier to be home than when at last he staggered through the front door of 1313 and shut it behind him.

Miri was sitting on the floor, coloring in her Unicorn Princess activity book. She noticed Danny and promptly released one of her trademark piercing screams.

"Miri? Miri! What's the matter?" called out Danny's mother from the kitchen. "Is something wrong?"

"ZOMBIE!" screeched Miri.

"No, Ma. It's just me," Danny answered, while giving Miri his dirtiest of looks. Miri responded by sticking out her tongue. "I tripped outside and got some scratches. Nothing serious. I'm going upstairs to wash up, ok?" He turned to Miri. "And you - stay out of my room," he whispered harshly. Miri pretended to ignore him and returned to her coloring. But when he was halfway up the stairs, she got him again. Only little sisters have that special skill of saying the most unhelpful and irritating things just so, and Miri was turning out to be an expert at it.

"Next time don't leave the window open, Danny. Robbers can come in!"

Danny froze. He was at a complete loss. How much did she know? What had she seen? The bottle of juice he had left behind...could she have tried some of it? He snuck a glance back at his sister. She was coloring innocently again, humming the theme song from the Princess Unicorn show.

"Just stay out of my room!" Danny repeated angrily.

He stormed up the rest of the stairs and locked the door to his room behind him. The bottle of pickle juice was on the desk, exactly where he had left it, right next to his school backpack. Danny picked it up and examined it closely. It seemed that there was the same amount of juice in it as when he had last seen it, but he could not be 100% sure. Maybe Miri had taken a little sip, maybe not. Knowing her, though, she probably would have spit it out right away. Miri was not a big pickle person. She certainly had not been flying around the house. Their mother definitely would have noticed that.

Danny put the bottle into his school backpack, then collapsed on his bed and exhaled deeply. An awful lot had happened since he had last been in his room. And, although it had started off great, most of the rest of it had been, well, awful.

He pulled his ruined shirt over his head and examined it in dismay. No way would his mother go for the excuse he had called out from the front hall. Best to hide the evidence in the usual way. He crumpled his shirt into a ball and leaned over to banish it to the furthest reaches of under-the-bed space. It was then that he once again detected the faint but unmistakable odor of sour pickles. The smell seemed to be originating from under his bed. What on earth could be causing that smell? Maybe Miri had spilled some of the juice there? Or, maybe he was just going crazy and smelling that stuff everywhere? He rolled off his bed to take a look.

A round greenish mass glowed faintly from the far corner. Danny groaned. More mysterious pickle stuff? What kind of trouble would this thing get him into? Well, ignoring it wasn't going to make it go away. He had better find out what it was. Danny reached behind him and pulled a baseball bat out of his closet. Holding it by the handle, he maneuvered the head of the bat behind the strange green orb and flicked it out from under the bed.

Danny's eyes brightened in recognition. The object, about the size and shape of a tennis ball, consisted of clothing, clothing that he recognized as his own. Specifically, the clothes that he had been wearing on the day he had discovered the pickle juice! He had tossed the juice-soaked clothes under his bed and forgotten about them. But something had happened to them. They seemed to have…changed.

Danny picked up the ball of clothing curiously and began to examine it. The dunking in the barrel must have caused the greenish discoloring, but what was really weird was the way the clothes were balled up so tightly. In fact, they were so compressed together that they formed an almost perfect sphere. All the different items of clothing flowed into each other. It was hard to tell where one article of clothing began and the next one ended. He could recognize the outlines of the clothes he had been wearing - even his sneakers, in a flattened sort of way, seemed to be a part of the ball. Danny tried to unpeel the ball by digging his fingers under what looked like a shirtsleeve, but found that he could barely lift the edge before it snapped back into position. He recalled how hard it had been to remove the clothing after they had been soaked in the pickle juice, and how they had begun to stick together even then. Somehow, the juice had caused his clothing to fuse together and form this tight ball. And now he was not strong enough to…

Danny smacked himself on the side of the head. Duh! If it was too hard for him to open, all he had to do was drink some pickle juice! Problem solved! He sipped half a mouthful from the bottle on his desk and picked up the ball again. This time, his fingers slid under the edge of the shirtsleeve as if they were gliding along the smoothest silk. He gripped the edge firmly with the fingers of both hands and gave a firm shake.

A wrinkled set of green clothing snapped out horizontally in front of him, stiff as a board. All the clothing was still attached together, forming a one-piece "suit" with a neck hole at one end and his sneakers at the other. Danny moved to lay it down on his bed, but one of the sneakers at the far end bumped against the side of his desk, whereupon the whole thing quivered and rolled itself back up into a ball. It reminded Danny very much of one of those snap wristbands that Miri and her friends had collected by the dozen the year before. The kind that was as straight as a ruler until you would strike it against your wrist, which made it collapse into a circular band.

Danny snapped open the sphere again and quickly stuck one arm into the neck hole. The movement caused the sneaker end to snap back as before, but Danny's hand inside the clothing blocked them from rolling up further than the suit's belt buckle. He stuck his other arm in as well, and then moved both of his arms back and sideways to try to stick them into the shirtsleeves. As soon as he did this, the bottom half of the suit, which his hands had been holding in place, snapped forward with great speed. Danny got a fleeting glimpse of the bottom of his sneakers headed rapidly at his face and then

WHAP!

Danny found himself sitting on the floor with a dull pain in his nose. He must have yanked his hands out of the clothing without realizing it because the suit was now completely balled up again on the floor next to him. Something wet was trickling down his face. He reached up to wipe it away and was very surprised to find blood on his fingers. This made no sense! Earlier that day a bullet hadn't even scratched him, and now a shoe to the face gives him a bloody nose? He was trying to puzzle this out when the front door banged open.

"Aliza! Danny! Miri! Come downstairs!" exclaimed Danny's father. "There's an amazing story they're going to be showing on Big Apple One!" Mr. Green headed straight for the big television set in the living room and flipped it on. Mrs. Green hurried in from the kitchen, followed by Miri. "What's happening? Is everything ok? Was there a terrorist attack?"

"No, no, nothing like that. I tried to call you from my cell when I got off the train, but my battery was dead." Mr. Green took the remote and flipped to the proper channel. Some cooking show was just ending, and a serious voice was intoning over the rolling credits.

"COMING UP NEXT ON THE SIX O'CLOCK NEWS. THE STORY OF THE CENTURY! ONLY HERE ON BIG APPLE ONE! STAY TUNED!"

"Oh, good, we're right on time. Danny!" Mr. Green shouted up the stairs. You don't want to miss this!"

Danny opened his door in time to hear Miri ask, "What's it about, Daddy?"

"Oh, something really exciting happened at the new branch today. I don't want to ruin the surprise, so let's just wait until they show it on the news. Come on, Danny!" Mr. Green shouted upstairs. "You're really going to get a kick out of this!"

Danny knew very well what the big news story was going to be about. His secret was about to be broadcast to the world! Well, there was nothing to do but face the music. Danny cleaned off his face with some tissues, barely noticing the abnormal speed with which his nosebleed had dried up. He threw on another shirt and headed downstairs, wondering if his parents would ever let him use the pickle juice again. It wasn't as if his experience with it so far had been such a resounding success.

The rest of his family took no notice as Danny edged into the living room. The six o'clock news had begun.

"GOOD EVENING. I'M STEVE MCLAIN WITH THE BIG APPLE ONE SIX O'CLOCK NEWS FOR WEDNESDAY, SEPTEMBER THE SEVENTH. OUR TOP STORY TONIGHT IS ABOUT AN UNKNOWN BOY, WHO FIRST RECOVERED A CHILD'S RUNAWAY BALLOON IN TRULY ASTOUNDING FASHION, THEN TOPPED THAT BY SINGLE-HANDEDLY PREVENTING A BANK ROBBERY IN BROOKLYN. FOLKS, YOU HAVE GOT TO SEE THIS TO BELIEVE IT. WE GO NOW TO THE ONLY KNOWN COMPLETE VIDEO RECORDING OF THE EVENT, CAPTURED EXCLUSIVELY FOR BIG APPLE ONE BY OUR REPORTER, BENJAMIN, um, BOWLAND."

In the Big Apple One newsroom, where the entire staff was watching the broadcast, Benjamin winced at the mispronunciation of his name. Well, at least they called him a reporter!

Danny slipped back out of the front room and into the kitchen. He wanted to enjoy his last few moments of privacy.

The video began playing. It sounded like the reporter had been filming him since he grabbed that balloon out of the air. He heard the whole bank robbery, listened to himself tell the thieves he would not drop the car, then the gasping of the crowd as he was shot. The part that he dreaded most was fast approaching. After the robbers had been caught, a reporter had shoved a camera straight in his face and asked him a bunch of questions. It must have been the same Benjamin person that took this video. As soon as his parents saw his face pop up onscreen, they would demand answers to those same questions, and make him tell them the secret. That should be happening just about now…

Miri squealed with delight.

"Look! Look at him, Mommy!"

"Why, that's…that's…"

Danny buried his face in his hands, wincing as he awaited the inevitable.

CHAPTER 5

THERE'S ALWAYS A PRICE TO PAY

"PRINCE CAPRICO!" shrieked Miri. "REEEEEEALY!"

"WHAT?!?" exclaimed Danny, as he bolted back into the front room.

He was just in time to see himself fly off into the sky, his back to the camera. Then the newsman's face appeared on the screen again.

"WELL, THERE YOU HAVE IT, FOLKS. POLICE OFFICIALS HAVE NO EXPLANATION FOR HOW THIS YOUNG MAN WAS ABLE TO ACCOMPLISH THESE AMAZING FEATS."

A close-up of the boy's face appeared on the screen. Miri screamed again, as only little girls can, and pointed excitedly. "It's the Prince! It's the Prince!"

Danny was flabbergasted. What in the world…? How was this possible?

"METROPOLITAN BANK HAS MADE AN OFFICIAL STATEMENT EXTENDING THEIR GRATITUDE TO THE BOY, WHO REMAINS ANONYMOUS AT THIS TIME.

POLICE AT THE SCENE HAD NO FURTHER COMMENTS, ALTHOUGH ONE OFFICER REMARKED THAT HE HOPED THE BOY WOULD REMAIN "ON OUR SIDE".

KEEP YOUR STATION TUNED TO BIG APPLE ONE, AS WE WILL KEEP YOU UPDATED ON ANY NEW INFORMATION RELATED TO NEW YORK'S UNKNOWN HERO..."

"Wow! That's some story!" remarked Mr. Green. He looked over at Danny, who was gaping at the screen. "Hey, Danny! Did you see all that? Wow. Incredible. Whoever he is, he's got to feel like the luckiest kid in the world. Imagine being able to do all that stuff, eh, Danny?"

Danny nodded without changing his expression.

Mrs. Green spoke up. "I don't know. I bet it's all a fake. I cannot believe anyone can really fly. This isn't just some publicity stunt your bank is running, is it, Jack?"

"Not that I know of, Aliza. The guys at the bank seemed pretty surprised by all this."

Miri certainly did not seem to have any doubts at all that her hero, Prince Caprico, had somehow appeared in the real world. Danny sometimes wondered whether Miri understood the concept that the Prince and his adventures were just supposed to be make-believe. She went skipping out of the room singing the Unicorn Princess song, a big fat happy smile on her face.

Danny finally recovered enough to break out of his stunned trance and flop onto the couch. He forced himself to focus, which seemed easier to do with the pickle juice still running through his system.

It made no sense, but it seemed that his secret was still

safe. For some unknown reason, the face that he had shown to the public earlier that afternoon had not been his own. Come to think of it, the Big Three hadn't recognized him either. Even if Shia did not know his name, he certainly should have remembered him from school. But none of them seemed to have had any idea who he was. Moreover, as much as he hated to admit it, Miri was right. That did look like Prince Caprico's face on the screen. What was that all about?

Danny lay face-up on the couch, pondering this latest and perhaps oddest twist. As he did so, the events of the past few days began churning through his mind. Without much conscious effort on his part, his brain shifted into a higher gear and began organizing and sorting everything that had happened since he had found the pickle juice, in an effort to find some explanations for what he had just seen. Danny felt barely in control of what was happening – it was as if he was just along for the ride. Images from the past few days flashed and whirled in front of him as his mind attempted to create logical connections between seemingly unrelated facts. The experience was similar to observing an expert detective sifting through information in order to crack a tough-to-solve case. It occurred to Danny that this newly discovered mental ability would be very useful for final exams. Except that he had decided not to waste the pickle juice on personal things like that…too bad…

Then it all clicked together. A solitary image was featured on his mental viewscreen. The illustration of the human head from the notebook he had found in the back of the basement.

Everything that the pickle juice enabled him to do seemed to work through his brain. The bullets did not harm him because he had focused on not getting hurt. And, from the moment he had flown out his bedroom window that afternoon, he had been worrying that people would recognize him. Somehow, his brain must be helping him with that, too!

Danny jumped off the couch and half-ran, half-flew down the hallway to the bathroom. His parents were startled by the small gust of wind caused by Danny's departure, but just shrugged their shoulders and returned their attention to the TV.

He locked the door behind him and stood in front of the mirror. What stared back at him was definitely not the TV star perfect face of Prince Caprico. Nope, just his regular-kid ordinary features, still quite dirty from his face-plant into Shia's backyard. But he wasn't trying not to be recognized. What if he did try…?

Before his eyes, his appearance wavered, then rippled. And a startling resemblance of the Prince appeared in the mirror.

Danny took a step back in surprise. That face in the mirror looked almost exactly like Prince Caprico. Even the hair was the same. He moved his hand up to feel his now-perfectly groomed head. However, his fingers did not feel his hair where the mirror showed it to be. Instead, his hand passed through the thick curly brown ringlets until it encountered what felt like his real hair underneath. Whoa. Danny moved his hands in and out of the layer of fake hair a few times, and then tried out the rest of his face. He quickly discovered that the "Prince" features were just a projection, a sort of virtual mask. There was no substance to it – his Danny Green face was there all along, invisible in the background. As this realization crossed his mind, the image in the mirror rippled again and Danny's real face became visible.

Incredible. He had the perfect disguise! No one would ever recognize him if he did not want them to! Assuming he could control it, of course. However, this did not seem to be a problem. By concentrating slightly, he found that he could shift his appearance back and forth between his normal face and his Prince face. This was just awesome. This pickle juice just kept on coming through with new ways to help. Maybe things were not so bad after all. But why Prince Caprico? Why was his face being replaced by a character from a kid's TV show?

While Danny idly shifted his face back and forth a few times, his brain powered back up into detective mode to solve this latest mystery. This time it did not take long. An image of the red balloon flashed up…he had been thinking about what Miri's reaction would be if she could see her brother zipping around the sky, something even her idol, the perfect-hair Prince couldn't do…then, trying to stop the robbery…concentrating on not being recognized….

That was it. Subconsciously, his mind had projected the perfect disguise - to appear as someone else completely. The last someone else he had been thinking about was Prince Caprico.

A loud KNOCK KNOCK on the bathroom door interrupted his train of thought.

"Who's in the bathroom?" whined Miri. "I have to go! Reeeeally!"

"It's me, Miri. I'll be out in a second." Danny made sure he had his Danny face on and opened the door.

Miri burst in glaring, her expression indicating that boys should not be allowed more than two minutes in bathrooms without prior written permission. "What are you waiting for?" she screeched. "Get out!"

Mike Petersen was having drinks and a light dinner with his golfing companions in the stately clubhouse adjoining the exclusive and well-kept Rockland golf course, a forty-five minute drive north from midtown Manhattan. The chief executive officers of two Wall Street investment banks had seemed to enjoy their game, and Stevens, one of his vice presidents, had not made nearly as much of a fool of himself as he usually did. Yes, the day had gone quite nicely. Petersen glanced up from his whisky sour during a lull in the boring story one of the CEOs had been sharing. There was a small but growing crowd gathered around the widescreen TV over the bar on the other side of the clubhouse dining room. His eyes narrowed when he spotted the familiar Big Apple One logo in the corner of the picture. The other executive, an annoyingly talented golfer named Goldman, had apparently been eyeing the hubbub at the bar as well, and remarked,

"Hey, Mike, isn't that your station's news broadcast? What's going on?"

"Nothing special that I am aware of. My people know to contact me immediately if anything of consequence were to occur." He turned to Stevens. "Stevens, anything newsworthy happen today? Did you get any calls from the office?"

"Uh, well, Dekel called about an hour ago, but it didn't sound important. And you were in the middle of putting."

"Hmmm," sniffed Mr. Petersen. The crowd around the TV was growing larger and more animated. Goldman excused himself and went over to check it out, followed by the other investment banker. Petersen waited a bit, then picked up his drink and ambled over, mostly succeeding in not allowing his curiosity to show.

The unruly horde at the bar was three deep by the time he arrived. He was just in time to see video footage of some kid "fly" up into the sky, followed by serious commentary from the newscaster, which he barely paid attention to. This pap, this drivel, was what the clowns at his station thought worthy of reporting? Treating cheap circus tricks as newsworthy enough for the lead story for the six o'clock broadcast? Big Apple One would be the laughingstock of the journalistic community! No one would take them seriously after this. Just wait until he found out who was responsible! He set the remainder of his drink down, motioned through the club's window to his waiting driver and walked briskly towards the exit.

"Petersen! Where you going?" called out Goldman behind him. "That was some story you guys ran! You knew about that kid? Why didn't you mention anything about it earlier?"

Mr. Petersen stopped and sighed to himself. He could not tell for sure whether Goldman had been mocking him or not. It would be best if he replied neutrally.

"Well, you know how it is. We need to check the accuracy of such stories before we go live with our broadcast. Which is why I've got to go. Such a story needs my personal attention." He managed to reach the door before Goldman could make any more snide comments. "I'll have my people call you tomorrow," he called out over his shoulder as he left hurriedly.

He would expose this boy for the fraud that he was. He would demonstrate how responsible journalism was conducted. Someone would pay for this embarrassment, of course. Oh, yes, someone would certainly pay.

The guards, usually calm and professional, seemed agitated that evening. From past experience, the prisoner knew that some important event had occurred in the outside world, something that could potentially disturb their master's grand plans. A pity. Accessing any further pigeon-provided video reports would be unwise for the next several days, as the guards would be extra vigilant.

The prisoner had once been a part of those grand plans, although he had not been aware of it at the time. He had been working on a rather radical method of increasing muscle function in individuals unfortunate enough to suffer from partial or even total paralysis, or from diseases such as muscular dystrophy. The idea was to develop a serum that would target the underused areas of the brain to enhance the mental signals that triggered muscle movement in the human body. His fellow researchers had dismissed his theories as science fiction, and the unpopularity of his approach quickly led to a serious lack of funding. He had been almost ready to give up when his bank had notified him that a sizeable sum had been wired in to his account, more than enough to allow him to continue his research for several months. He had received similar amounts every three months for over a year before his unknown benefactor had finally made an appearance.

A long black limousine had pulled up outside his nondescript laboratory on the outskirts of the quiet upstate village of Ellenville, New York that day, a little over twenty years ago by his reckoning. The driver, a heavyset but nimble fellow, had rushed to open the rear door, out of which appeared a distinguished silver-tipped cane, brandished by a very confident-seeming individual with slick-backed dark hair and mirrored sunglasses. The man had been wearing a well-made Italian suit that looked like it had cost well into the four digits. Another bulky but solid-looking individual, clearly a bodyguard of some sort, followed him out of the limo. The man with the cane was clearly a figure of some importance.

He had observed the proceedings from his office window, not realizing the men were there for him until the he heard the firm, insistent pounding on the lab's front door. The bodyguard's meaty fist was making quite a racket. He could not fathom what these men wanted with him. Maybe they had the wrong address?

As soon as he opened the front door, the men had swept inside as if they owned the place. It turned out that they did, to some extent. The man with the cane had headed straight for his office, and promptly made himself at home by sitting down in the only chair in the room. The driver and bodyguard took up positions on either side of him.

"Dr. Joseph Picolo, right? Let me introduce myself. My name is John Simonelli."

Simonelli's voice had a nasal city twang to it that belied the sophisticated image he was clearly trying to project. The prisoner remembered that this had made him extremely uneasy and suspicious. The name "Simonelli" had also sounded familiar, and not in a positive way. He just could not place where he had heard it before.

"I'm Dr. Picolo. Do I know you?"

"Now you do. Your bank account knows me for a while already. That cash didn't just get there by magic, ya know."

"Ah. So, you are my secret benefactor. Well, thank you, Mr. Simonelli. Thank you very much! I doubt I could have continued my research without you!"

"Yeah, about that research. How's it goin'?"

"Very promising. I think I'm on the verge of a major breakthrough."

"And how long until you have a, what you would call, a finished product?"

"I'll probably have a test worthy sample in a month or so..."

"Excellent, doc, excellent. So, I'll expect delivery in a month."

"Delivery? What do you mean?"

"Doctor, Doctor. I'm as charitable as the next guy, but I also expect some return on my investments. I'll be back to collect the product when it's ready. And Doctor," Mr. Simonelli got up from his chair and pointed his cane at Joseph's nose. "Please do not disappoint me. I'm expecting great things from you."

Mr. Simonelli and his men had left soon after, but Joseph Picolo's long nightmare had only just begun. He should have realized that the old saying was true - nothing ever comes for free. All that money he had been getting was just Mr. Simonelli's way of seizing control of his experimental serum. It was when he came across a newspaper article about suspected members of the New York Mafia a few days later that he realized just how much trouble he might be in. Apparently, his benefactor was an alleged mid-level Mafia boss. A "rising star" in fact, known for his ruthlessness and cruelty to those who crossed him. The expensive suits and fancy cane, as Picolo would learn all too well, were just window dressing, an attempt by Simonelli to be seen as a gentleman, a sophisticate. Underneath it all, he was just a common thug, albeit more successful than most.

At first, Dr. Picolo could not understand what Mr. Simonelli could have wanted with his serum. Did he have some relative with paralysis, perhaps? As he got closer to finalizing his experiments, however, it occurred to him that while someone with damaged nerves and muscles would certainly benefit from his invention, he had never considered what the effect on a healthy human's muscles would be. Maybe Mr. Simonelli had jumped to the reasonable conclusion that his formula would boost an average person as well, making him or her stronger and faster. Such an invention would be in great demand and very profitable.

If Mr. Simonelli and his "family" controlled the product, they could make untold amounts of money, making them ever more powerful.

Although his initial assumptions turned out to be partially correct, the real truth about Mr. Simonelli's interest in his serum turned out to be far more disturbing and sinister…

A sudden commotion outside of his cell broke the prisoner's train of thought. The guards scrambled to stand at attention. He could hear the jingling of keys and the sound of iron gates opening and closing. Then a man in an expensive suit stood outside his cell, silver-tipped cane tapping on the bars.

"So, Doctor. After all these years, it seems that someone may have found your formula. We need to talk."

"Ok, that's all for now," said Uncle Dan.

"Wait, wait. So this prisoner is the guy who made the pickle juice?"

"Sorry – time for bed, Tommy. Remember, I told you we wouldn't have time for questions tonight."

"But how did it end up in Danny's basement? Is Mr. Simonelli going to try to steal it?"

Uncle Dan tapped his watch. "Story's over for tonight. See you next week."

"Hmpf," grumbled Tommy, rolling over in his blanket.

His dreams that night were certainly more entertaining than usual. They may have even involved a bit of flying.

CHAPTER 6

A HERO IS BORN

Tommy's parents could not get over how eagerly Tommy got ready for bed, but they certainly were not complaining. Uncle Dan showed up right on time, ushered them out the door, and headed up to Tommy's room. Tommy was certainly glad to see him. He had had a whole week to think about the story so far, and was impatient to get started.

"Ok, Uncle Dan, you're up to where the prisoner was talking to the guy with the cane – Mr. Simon-something."

"That's Simonelli, Tommy."

"Right. So tell me more about that part. Did Mr. Simonelli try to steal the formula from Dr. Pickles? Is he going to try to steal it from Danny, too?"

"Hold on there, Tommy. First of all, it's Dr. Picolo. Second of all, I thought you didn't like the parts about the prisoner. As I recall, you called them "boring".

Tommy was a little red-faced. "Well, that was in the beginning. Those parts are much better now..."

"You mean, now that you know more of the story. Well, I'm glad you realize that each part of the story must be told in its proper place for everything to make sense. Trust me. In the end, all your questions will be answered. For now, we'll have to go back to Danny for a while and see how he's handling everything."

Danny once again found it difficult to fall asleep that night. He awoke the next morning groggy and late, with barely enough time to get to school. As he quickly threw on his shirt and pants, he spotted the green clothes-ball in the corner of his room. It must have rolled there after smacking him in the face the day before. Well, he could not leave it around for his mother to discover. Besides, an interesting idea had occurred to him about a possible use for the pickle juice suit. He scooped the ball up, stuffed it in his backpack next to the bottle of pickle juice, and headed down the stairs towards the front door. He turned to say goodbye to his mother, who was fixing Miri's hair as she ate breakfast. From what he could see of the kitchen table, Miri was planning to bring every Prince Caprico item she owned to school that day.

The school playground was buzzing by the time Danny showed up. Everyone was excitedly discussing the amazing story they had seen on the news the night before.

"Did you see the way he was able to zoom off into the sky? Man, I'd give anything to be able to do that!"

"Wasn't it cool the way those bullets didn't hurt him at all?"

"I can't believe I missed that! I live right around the corner from that bank!"

"I wonder who he is? He's, like, the luckiest kid in the world!"

Danny's face flushed red as he made his way through the yard. They were talking about him! And nobody had any idea. Well, nobody except for...

"Hey Danny! There you are! We think you have some explaining to do!"

Sammy and Joe were headed towards him determinedly. Danny motioned them over to a quiet corner of the playground so they would not be overheard.

"Ok, Danny," began Joe. "You're the only one we know that can do anything like this flyboy kid. So what's going on? Who was that on the news yesterday?"

"Uh, that was me."

"Yeah, you wish, Danny," said Sammy. "You don't look anywhere near as cool as that guy. My little sister thinks it was Prince whatshisname from that Unicorn Girly Princess show. So come on. Do you know anything about it?"

"Really, guys. It was me. As you said, do you know anyone else who can do this stuff? You don't have to believe me if you don't want to, but that's your problem."

Sammy and Joe looked at each other skeptically. "So why didn't it look like you?" asked Joe.

"Well, you know I didn't want anyone to recognize me, right? So the pickle juice throws up some kind of camouflage face so that no one knows who I am."

Joe was still having some doubts. "Okay, and how did

Prince Wonderful's face get picked for the job? Are you, like, a big fan or something?" he snorted derisively.

Danny sighed. "I guess I was thinking about how dumb it was that my sister Miri is in awe of that guy, and his face must've been in my head when I was trying not to be recognized."

Joe and Sammy did not seem entirely convinced by this argument, but before they could question Danny further, a late-model bright red convertible roared up in front of the schoolyard. The Big Three had arrived. Joe tapped Sammy on the shoulder as a skinny boy ran toward the vehicle.

"Looks like the little rat is providing curbside service now. Just unbelievable!"

Martin hurried to open the sports car's rear door for Shia and his gang. Danny noticed that Martin had upgraded his notepad to a more official-looking clipboard. Probably with a list of people who had not paid up yet. Like him.

Unfortunately for Martin, his efforts to impress went completely unappreciated. Shia emerged purposefully from the back seat and brushed right past the waiting Martin and his clipboard. The poor boy was then nearly trampled by Mike and Ox, who strode out right behind their leader. Shia marched importantly to the center of the yard and cleared his throat loudly. "Listen up, everyone!" bellowed Ox. "The Man has something to say!"

The playground quieted noticeably. Whether they wanted to or not, the boys knew they had better listen to Shia's latest pronouncement.

Shia had an unnaturally large smile plastered across his face. He grandly spread out his arms and began to speak. "I'm sure everyone's heard about this freako kid who's all over the news. He stops bank robbers, he can fly, blah, blah, blah. Well, and you heard it from me first, he's nothing special. He's just some punk kid they're making a big deal out of."

Subdued gasps of disbelief sounded throughout the playground. Sammy and Joe turned to Danny, who shrugged his shoulders.

Shia continued. "Yeah, this hotshot kid landed in my backyard yesterday, and me and my boys wiped the floor with him. The big baby even started to cry!"

"Wah wah wah. Boo hoo hoo!" chanted Mike and Ox. Then the Big Three high-fived each other, laughing uproariously.

"Oh, yeah, that," muttered Danny.

"That really happened? They're telling the truth?" exclaimed Sammy.

"Well, sort of. I ran out of juice at the wrong time and I ended up in their backyard. They kicked me around a little."

"But why didn't they recognize you?" asked Joe.

"Like I told you, the juice disguises my face. It must have still been working a little when they saw me."

The Big Three triumphantly fist-bumped each other for a while, then marched into the school building. Even though not everyone completely believed Shia's story, the excited, hopeful mood that the unknown flying boy and his amazing feats had generated had been punctured like a busted balloon. The kids in the playground wandered around listlessly until the bell rang, then began to file quietly inside.

Sammy and Joe turned back to Danny. Their faces had

the same let-down, dejected expression as everyone else's.

"What? What's with the look, guys?" exclaimed Danny. "I'm just happy I didn't get killed yesterday! I did fall out of the sky, you know!"

Joe scuffed his shoe on the ground. "I guess it's annoying to watch those jerks walk around like kings of the world when you could just, well…"

"Just what? Drink some pickle juice and go beat them up? I'm not going to waste this stuff on these punks, I told you. Besides, people might figure out who I am if I suddenly started doing things like that."

"I guess he has a point, Joe," said Sammy. Let's lay off him a little."

Joe mumbled reluctantly in agreement, and the boys joined the quiet mass of children as they made their way into the school building.

The somber mood lasted throughout the day. None of the boys felt like talking much as they made their way home. After they walked a few blocks in relative silence, Sammy tried to lighten things up. "So, did you see the way Shia just brushed off Martin before? He kept on trying to give Shia his snitch list, but Shia was too busy showing off about beating Danny up! Oops. Sorry, Danny."

"It's ok, Sammy."

Joe grunted. "But tomorrow, or maybe the day after, Shia will remember to ask who hasn't paid up. What are you gonna do then, Danny? You're gonna actually pay that creep?"

Danny did not know what to say. He had so much power at his disposal, yet it was useless in this situation.

"Let's talk about something else for a while, ok, guys? I've had enough Shia for today."

"Good idea! Let's talk about those Mets!" exclaimed Sammy.

Danny and Joe groaned. Sammy tended to get a little too enthusiastic about his favorite baseball team, but anything was better than discussing their problems with the Big Three.

"I have a better idea," broke in Joe. "And it's sort of important."

"What?" asked Danny.

"What do you want people to call you? Next time you go out and use your pickle juice, I mean. When people ask you who you are, you should have something to tell them. Not just "Unknown Flying Kid," like they said on the news."

"Hmm. Good point. I never thought about that," said Danny.

"Hey! How about UFB?" exclaimed Sammy.

Danny and Joe stared at him

"You know, as in, Unidentified Flying, uh, Boy?" Sammy saw the look on his friends' faces and winced. "Ohhhh-kay, I guess not, then," he trailed off.

"Bulletproof Kid?" suggested Joe. How about Mystery Boy?"

"Mystery Boy. I like that one," remarked Sammy.

"I don't know. It's ok, I guess. I'm not doing this to be famous or anything, you know."

"But you still need to be able to tell them something. Or someone's going make up some really dumb name that you're gonna be stuck with forever."

The boys spent the rest of their walk trying to come up with something catchy that didn't sound too lame. However, nothing had really clicked by the time they got to the corner of East 13th Street. Danny was about to head on down his block when Joe said,

"Uh, Danny? Wait up. See those people going into Marty's? Are they the ones you told us about?"

Danny turned to look. Two familiar men wearing leather jackets and sunglasses were entering the store.

"Those are the guys who shot Mr. Marty!" whispered Danny.

"You sure?" asked Joe.

"Absolutely. And now I can do something about it!"

"Awesome!" exclaimed Sammy. "We're gonna get to see some Mystery Boy action!" He began looking up and down the block urgently.

"What are you doing?" asked Joe.

"Well, Danny needs a place to drink his pickle juice and get his face changed. He can't do that in the middle of the sidewalk. People will notice."

"So what are you looking for?"

"A phone booth, of course."

"Why? People can see into a phone booth too!"

"You know, I never thought of that."

"Guys! Over here," called Danny. "I found a place."

Danny was rummaging through his backpack in a small alleyway between Marty's and the pizza place next door. Sammy and Joe hurried over to join him.

Joe got there first, just in time for Danny to hand him a strange green ball. "Hold this a second, will you?" Danny asked. Then Danny dug out his bottle of pickle juice and gulped down several ounces, just to be sure. Running out of steam fifty feet up in the air was not something he wanted to have to go through again.

As Sammy and Joe watched, the air in front of Danny's face shimmered. It reminded Joe of the wavy airspace right above a campfire or a hot barbeque grill. And then the face they had seen in the news was staring back at them.

"Incredible!" breathed Sammy.

"Pretty cool, Danny," said Joe. "Now, what's with this ball you gave me?"

"Well, basically it's a set of clothes that got dunked in pickle juice by mistake. It gave me a bloody nose yesterday when it snapped back in my face – and this was while I was powered up."

"That's one tough set of clothes."

"Exactly. So if it's tough enough to hurt me, maybe it

also won't get shredded by bullets, like my shirt did yesterday."

"Hey – that could be like a uniform for you! You know, like you'd put it on whenever you go out to do your thing!" exclaimed Sammy.

"Uh, yeah, I guess so," answered Danny. "I just need something to protect my clothes, though. Anyway, I've got to figure out how to get it on, and it might not be easy. Joe, can you keep a lookout? Let me know if those guys leave the store."

"Sure, Danny."

Danny snapped open the green suit of clothing as he had the day before, and held it horizontally out in front of him. How to get into it before it snapped back? He would have to move very quickly. But that should not be a problem. Yesterday he had zipped out to the Atlantic Ocean in just a few minutes! He carefully curled the fingers of each hand around opposing sides of the green suit's neck-hole, pulled then apart slightly to widen the opening, then yanked his legs off the ground and jammed them straight through the hole. He had moved so fast and with such force that his shoe-covered feet pushed all the way through the pant legs and down into the green-stained sneakers at the end of the suit. After that, it was a simple matter to put his arms through the sleeves. The whole process had taken just over a second.

Danny looked down at himself. The green clothing was very wrinkled, and it was not a fashion statement by any means. It did fit nice and snug over his regular clothes, though. Even the green-stained sneakers at the bottom had stretched to cover his school shoes. Not bad. "Guys, what do you think?" he asked, raising his head.

Sammy stared at him in awe. "Wow, Danny. You look…wow."

Joe turned to see what Sammy was wowing at and took a step backward, eyes widening.

"Whoa, man."

Joe was not impressed easily. Now he seemed almost…*intimidated* by Danny.

It was not just Joe and Sammy. Danny also noticed some differences. The effects of the pickle juice seemed more intense, more concentrated. He felt even more focused, with an even greater sense of strength and confidence, than he did the other times. What had changed?

Danny noticed a dull, cracked mirror in a broken frame leaning against the alley wall and went over to get a good look at himself. The green clothes, although extremely wrinkled, appeared to fit him very well. They also seemed to be glowing more deeply than before he put them on. It was as if the combination of the juice inside him and the juice absorbed in the clothes were working together. It certainly felt that way. Danny shivered with excitement. Who knew what he was capable of now? The only downside was that these clothes make him look a little funny. Almost like...

"I look like a giant pickle!"

"S-sort of, yeah," stammered Joe. Joe never stammered. And he was still staring wide-eyed at Danny.

"Are you ok?" asked Danny. "Why are you looking at me like that?"

"I don't know. You look different in that suit. Not just because of your face. I – I can't explain it."

"He looks…heroic. That's the word. Heroic," Sammy

whispered.

Danny blushed. "I'm not anything like that. I just want to do what's right. I bet anyone else would do the same thing if they had found the juice. Well, most people, anyway," he added, as thoughts of Shia and his goons crossed his mind.

"Hey! I got it!" Sammy almost shouted.

"What?'

Sammy pointed dramatically at Danny.

"PICKLE BOY!"

"That's retarded."

"No, wait," Joe interjected. "That's not half-bad."

"Huh?" grunted Danny skeptically. "You *like* the name Pickle Boy?"

"Well, you said it yourself. You do look like one in that outfit."

"And," broke in Sammy, sniffing the air near Danny, "Just like in the birthday song, YOU SMELL LIKE ONNNNNE, TOOOOO! Thank you, thank you very much-ah." Sammy bowed grandly.

Danny turned back to the mirror. "Pickle Boy, huh?"

Sammy was still in his bow and had been facing the alley entrance. Suddenly he began pointing excitedly. "Hey, look! There go those guys from the store!" he squeaked.

"Great! Now I'm gonna let them have it," Danny exclaimed, pounding his fists together. He began to move past

Joe toward the alley entrance.

"Hold on a second, Danny," said Joe, grabbing Danny's arm. "Is this what you really want to do?"

"What do you mean? Why not?"

'Well, I was just thinking. What are you planning to do to these guys?"

"I don't know. Knock them around a little? Bring them to the police?"

"But how about the people that sent them? They'll probably just send someone else to collect from Mr. Marty."

"Hmmm." said Danny.

"Not only that," continued Joe, "their boss or whoever sent them will think Mr. Marty snitched on them, and probably do something really nasty."

"Maybe burn down his store," added Sammy.

"Or worse," Joe added.

Danny was getting frustrated. "So what should I do? Right now they're getting away! And they probably just took more money from Marty's!"

"Let them," said Joe.

"Are you nuts? Why would I do that?"

"Because you can find out what they're doing with that money. Find out where they're going with it."

Danny's eyes lit up. "Right. I can follow them until I

find out who sent them. If I can take their boss down, nobody will bother the Martys anymore!" He stuck out his hand to Joe. "Thanks! Great idea!"

"Glad to help!" Joe smiled. And Joe did not smile that often, either. But his grin turned into a grimace as Danny shook his hand and almost yanked his shoulder out of its socket.

Sammy was watching this exchange with some bewilderment. "How did you figure all this out, Joe? And when did you become such a crime expert?"

"I read a lot of mystery stories. You should come with me to the library sometimes instead of playing all those video games."

There was a sudden gust of air as Danny launched himself upwards. He stopped and turned when he cleared the tops of the buildings to wave at his friends. "See you guys later!"

"GO, PICKLE BOY!" Sammy shouted after him.

Danny shot up high enough so that the two men, who were getting into their parked car, would not easily be able to spot him. The vehicle pulled away and Danny followed at a distance, being careful not to lose track of it as the car blended into traffic. He hoped it would not take that long to get to where they were going. His mother would be expecting him home for supper.

It had not been a fun day at Big Apple One. Mr. Petersen had stormed in at eight o'clock in the morning looking like he was ready to kill someone. He had immediately summoned the department heads for an hour-long closed-door meeting in the main conference room, during which he had ranted and raved about the poor judgment and lousy journalism skills exhibited by the entire office in the handling of the flying boy affair. How irresponsible it was for a respected organization like Big Apple One to fall for cheap party tricks. A boy soaring through the skies? Stopping bullets? Obviously an elaborate hoax. If by some remote chance there was some truth to the story, well, the thought of such power in the hands of a small child should be a cause of great concern to the general public, not a reason for sensationalist excitement. Mr. Petersen had concluded his pronouncements by threatening to fire or demote everyone involved unless the truth was uncovered, and quickly.

Benjamin, having been on staff for less than a week, had obviously not been invited, but as the red-faced executives and senior staff exited the meeting and began to relay Mr. Petersen's instructions to their subordinates, many annoyed and accusing glances were aimed in his direction. Eventually, Bob felt sorry for him and pulled him into a corner to explain the situation.

"He thinks it's all a trick? That's ridiculous! I was right there!"

Bob sighed. "I don't understand his attitude. Maybe he's upset that it was released without his approval."

"But he wasn't around! And we tried to reach him!"

"I know, kid. Look, don't let it discourage you. It's not always like this. Go on out there and find some other story." Bob waved his hand in a little half-circle. "Maybe keep away from this flying boy stuff for awhile, though. Petersen's really on the warpath about that particular item."

Benjamin was not a happy person. What was supposed to be his lucky break had just gotten everyone at the station in trouble, and probably made them all hate him. Well, there was nothing that could be done about that now. He had to suck it up and get over it. He would go out there with his camera, just as Bob suggested. But he would not take all of Bob's advice. Benjamin had been the one to discover the kid, and he was determined to be the one that found out the truth behind this mystery boy. Who was he? Where did he get these incredible abilities? And, why did he smell like sour pickles, of all things?

Benjamin was gathering his equipment and preparing to head out when a uniformed police officer entered the newsroom. Benjamin recognized him – it was the cop that he had interviewed briefly following the bank robbery, right after their flyboy had disappeared. The officer scanned the room, his mouth set grimly. After a few seconds, his eyes settled on Benjamin.

"You there. I'm Officer Thompson, NYPD. You were the reporter who discovered this, uh, mystery boy, right? I need you to come down to the station to answer a few questions."

"Is there a problem, Officer? Am I in trouble?"

"Well, the Captain wants to find out any information he can about this kid. As you probably got closer to him than anyone else, he'd appreciate your making a brief appearance at the precinct."

"Um, ok, I guess..."

"Of course he'll go with you, Officer," broke in the smooth rich TV voice they all knew so well. Mr. Petersen himself had come up behind Benjamin and clapped him on the shoulder. "In fact, I might as well join you. It's important that the police get to the bottom of this. Either this story is one of the biggest hoaxes in recent memory, or even worse," Mr. Petersen paused dramatically, "it's real. A mere child with that kind of ability." He shuddered. "Either way, we'll help you get to the truth. Won't we, son?" he asked, flashing Benjamin his famous broadcaster smile.

This time it was Benjamin who shuddered. That was the most artificial smile he had ever witnessed.

CHAPTER 7

THE COVER COMES OFF

Danny checked his watch for the third time. He had been following the men in their silver Mercedes from above for over an hour, all the while trying not to be spotted. The thugs had made two other stops after Marty's, one at a pizza place and the other at a liquor store. Danny had avoided flying out in the open, zipping from rooftop to rooftop whenever possible, reasoning that if people noticed him and started pointing, it would alert the bad guys to his presence. So far, he had been mostly successful. It was getting late, though, and he did not want his mother to start wondering where he was. He hoped that the men would reach their final destination soon.

He was currently on the roof of a run-down townhouse in a seedy section of East Flatbush. Split-open garbage bags were strewn everywhere, and Danny was being subjected to a city-special summer day perfume combination of rotting trash and hot rooftop tar. He had landed here because the Mercedes had stopped across the street in front of a boarded-up building that was even more decrepit than the structure he was on top of.

Danny crouched down behind the ledge at the edge of the

roof and peeked over. The shiny luxury car looked decidedly out of place in front of the neglected property, whose windows and doorways were covered with graffiti-stained wooden slats. The rest of the houses on the block were in similar shape, which gave the whole street a sad, forlorn appearance. A huge, dark-skinned man, bare chest and arms rippling with muscles, leaned casually against the wall of the building, designer sunglasses hiding his eyes. A half-destroyed public phone stand that was stationed on the sidewalk right in front of the building's boarded-up front door was the only other notable object in sight.

What were these men doing, stopping in the middle of nowhere? Danny waved some flies away from his face and tapped his foot impatiently. He had to go to the bathroom, and the smell was getting him nauseous. But he owed it to Mr. Marty to stick it out. After all, he could not expect the bad guys to just lead him right to their boss, nice and easy. That only happened on TV shows…

A movement out of the corner of his eye. The bare-chested guy was standing up and was giving the "ok" sign to the parked Mercedes. A moment later, the men exited the vehicle, each of them glancing up and down the street, before heading directly towards the boarded up building. Danny raised his eyebrows in surprise. He was even more surprised when a heavy slab of wood, which had seemed to be bolted over the front door of the building, slid aside as the men approached, and then closed smoothly back into place as soon as the men were inside.

Ok, that was definitely unusual. It reminded Danny of the secret door in his basement. Secret doors meant there was something hidden on the other side. So that meant…this might be what he was looking for! Maybe those men were reporting to their boss here! Then he could go in there and…and…

Danny turned away from the ledge to think this through. He was not too worried about getting hurt, but he didn't have any real experience dealing with criminals. Even the bank robbers he had stopped the day before had, at the end, been caught by the police, not by him. Perhaps it would be a good idea to get the police involved here, too. But how? Should he fly off, find a patrol car, and try to persuade the officers to come back with him? It might take too long, and maybe they would not even listen to him. How could he convince the cops that it was an emergency?

Emergency. Of course! Every kid knew to dial 911 in an emergency. Too bad his parents thought he was too young to have his own cell…but how about that phone booth down below? It did not look promising, but maybe it was still working.

He peered over the edge of the roof again. The big goon with the sunglasses was more alert now, and was obviously on lookout duty. There was no way he would be looking out for some kid in a green suit, though. Danny waited until the man turned to face away from him, then quickly hopped over the edge of the roof and let himself fall to the ground below, floating upwards slightly at the end so that he would land gently and silently.

A pigeon landed on top of the phone booth and turned its expectant eyes on Danny.

The lookout was still facing the boarded-up building, so Danny nonchalantly strolled across the street to the phone kiosk and tentatively picked up the battered receiver. A dial tone!

The lookout man turned at the sound. "What the…where did you come from, kid? It don't matter. Beat it!"

"But I have to make a phone call! It's an emergency!"

Up close, the thug appeared as if he had stepped straight out of the screen of some very violent video game. Even his muscles seemed to have muscles. He took off his sunglasses and glared at Danny. "What's the emergency? And what's with the funky clothes? You with the circus or somethin'?"

Danny put on his best sad face. "I think I'm lost!" he whimpered. "I have to call my parents!"

"Fine, kid. Whatever. Just get it over with and disappear!"

The lookout headed back to his spot next to the building. "Stupid kid," he muttered to himself. Danny turned back to the phone and dialed 911.

"911, what is your emergency?"

"Yes. I just saw two men who robbed a grocery store go into an old apartment building. I think it's their hideout!"

The lookout stopped in his tracks and whirled around.

"Who is this? Who's calling? Is this a joke?" asked the operator. "You could get in a lot of trouble for this, young man!"

"No joke, ma'am. I'm calling you because they hurt a really nice man I know, and now I'm going to find out who sent them. And when I do, they're gonna be really sorry. You might want to send some police cars."

The lookout was big, but he was not stupid. This kid was obviously trouble. Nostrils flaring, he charged at Danny like a crazed bull. "Gimme that phone!" he bellowed.

Danny eyed the onrushing thug. Last week, faced with this situation, he would have ruined his underwear. Things were very different now. As Mr. Muscles was about to find out.

"I'm sorry. Who is this?!?" repeated the operator.

Mr. Muscles lunged, arms like tree trunks reaching for Danny's face.

"One second, please," said Danny.

Danny stuck his fist out, connecting solidly with Muscles' upper chest. The bone-cracking force of the blow drove the thug head over heels through the air until his sizable bulk met the side of the apartment building. As the lookout's unconscious body thudded to the ground, Danny cleared his throat, slightly embarrassed at what he was about to declare.

"Um, this is uh, Pickle Boy."

"What? Speak up, son. I can't hear you."

Danny gathered his self-confidence and repeated it with greater conviction.

"Pickle Boy. The kid who stopped those bank robbers yesterday. You can call me PICKLE BOY!"

Officer Thompson was relieved when he finally pulled into the 70th precinct's parking lot and escorted the Bowman kid and his boss inside the station. He was aware that Mr. Petersen was an important newsperson, but did not understand why the man resented the flying kid so much. Mr. Petersen had made his opinion of the whole matter very clear during the trip to the precinct, while the young reporter who had "discovered" the boy sat silently in the corner of the cruiser's back seat. Well, thought Thompson, it was out of his hands now. He marched them to the captain's office and knocked on the frosted glass door, upon which was stenciled "Captain Fazio" in solid black letters.

"Come in," barked a gruff voice.

Mr. Petersen took the liberty of going in first, much to the annoyance of Officer Thompson, who did not have much use for self-important people. Behind a cluttered desk sat a short but well-built man with a full head of jet-black hair, who, upon noticing Petersen, grimaced in distaste.

"So, Petersen, here to make us look bad again? Where's that reporter who talked to the flying kid? Him, I wanna talk to."

"My job is simply to report the facts, Captain," Mr. Petersen replied with a tight smile.

"The way you see the facts, anyway," muttered Captain Fazio, who spotted Benjamin attempting to squeeze into the office behind Petersen. "Son, come on in. Sit down."

Benjamin tentatively took the offered seat across the desk from the Captain. There was another empty chair next to Benjamin's, but Mr. Petersen was not invited to make use of it. After a few awkward seconds, he did so anyway. Officer Thompson smirked and backed out of the office, closing the door behind him.

"So, young man," said the Captain in his most reassuring voice. "They say you're the one who saw this kid first. What can you tell me about him?"

Mr. Petersen put his hand on Benjamin's shoulder. "Captain, I have reason to suspect that young Benjamin here was the victim of a hoax. Surely you don't believe a boy can fly, do you? I mean, most of them can't even jump very high. It's simply ludicrous..."

The Captain made a great effort to control his temper, and turned his gaze from Benjamin to glare at the newsman. "If you don't mind, Petersen, I asked this gentleman a question, and I'd like to hear him answer it. I have too many eyewitnesses to just… ignore the whole situation, as you obviously want to do." Turning back to Benjamin, he continued. "Go on, son. What did you see?"

As Benjamin related his account of the bank robbery to Captain Fazio, Officer Thompson was catching up on the gossip around the station. Making his way past the 911 dispatch area, he noticed one of the operators staring at her phone in some confusion.

"What kind of name is Pickle Boy?" she said, shaking her head, hanging up the phone. "Probably some prank caller."

Something clicked in Officer Thompson's head. "Who was that? What was that call about?"

"Some crazy kid. He said he found some people who stole money from some guy he knows, and it sounded like he wanted to go into their hideout and beat them up."

"What did he say his name was again?"

"I think he said Pickle Boy. You can check the recording. Can you believe that?"

"Hmmm." Thompson thought for a moment. "Pickle Boy. Pickle Boy, Pickle Boy, Pickle Boy. I wonder if he smells like pickles, too." He peered over the operator's shoulder. "Where did that call come from?"

The operator pointed the location out on the map displayed on her computer screen. "That's a rough part of town," she commented.

"No normal kid would have a reason for being there. We

may not be dealing with a normal kid, though. I'd better inform the Captain."

Benjamin had managed to get most of his story out, despite frequent interruptions by Mr. Petersen. After describing how the gunmen's bullets had no effect on the boy, Captain Fazio had remarked that he could use a kid like that on the force. Mr. Petersen promptly exploded with indignation that the police would even consider giving an untrained child such responsibility.

"Relax, Petersen. It was just a joke, all right? We don't have any uniforms that fit him, anyway." A hurried knocking on the door halted Petersen's retort in its tracks.

"What now?" sighed Fazio. Thompson stuck his head in. "Captain, the 911 lines just got a call from some kid calling himself Pickle Boy."

The Captain rolled his eyes. "And this is important, why?"

"He smelled like sour pickles," Benjamin whispered wonderingly.

"Who did?" scowled Fazio.

"The boy from yesterday's robbery," Thompson answered, nodding at Benjamin. "Get this, Captain. He said he was about to break into some criminal hideout, and suggested we send police backup! I think this might be the same kid!"

Petersen turned to Fazio. "Captain, in all seriousness, there is the possibility that this "Pickle Boy" is just some kid trying to play hero. Maybe he just got lucky at the bank yesterday. That boy could be in grave danger if he tries to go up against hardened thugs. I think it's time we put an end to this little game, and perhaps save this foolish child's life, if we're not too late."

Captain Fazio chewed on a fingernail for a moment, and then turned back to Benjamin. "What about you, son? You think this is all some game?"

Benjamin glanced at Mr. Petersen. He knew his boss would not like his answer, but he felt he had to be truthful to the Captain.

"I – I think the kid's for real. I was right there. I know what I saw."

The Captain sighed heavily and looked back and forth between Benjamin and his boss. After a moment or two, he came to a decision and stood up. "Well, either way, he's asking for a lot of trouble. Thompson, let's gather some troops and get to the bottom of this." He reached for his hat and uniform jacket and headed for the door. "Let's go, people. You're all coming with me. I'm responding to this call myself!"

With a slight flex of his legs, Danny performed a standing jump from the phone kiosk to the bolted-over door of the building, a distance of about twenty feet. He stood there for a moment, sizing up the heavy wooden plank covering the opening. It probably would not open up for him, as it did for the two men earlier. Danny would have to get it open by himself. This should not be much of a problem, though. He did not know exactly how strong he was, but if lifting a car was a piece of cake, this should not be too hard, either.

Danny extended his arms, grasped the plank with both hands, set himself, and yanked hard. With a scream of tearing metal, the entire piece was violently ripped out of its frame, bolts and all. Danny, taken by surprise, lost his grip on the door, which shot over his head and tumbled end over end behind him, finally coming to rest in the middle of the street. Wow, thought Danny, eyeing the damage. Wow. A huge smile crossed his face. This pickle juice was AWESOME!

He turned back to the now-open doorway and surveyed the dimly lit interior, grin fading quickly. He was not here to have fun. He was here because of what those monsters did to Mr. Marty. Now he was going to make sure they would pay for it.

Face set determinedly, Danny stepped inside the building.

Followed shortly by the pigeon.

Uncle Dan looked at his watch.

“Don’t even think about it!” threatened Tommy.

“Ok, ok,” laughed Uncle Dan. “You were in bed early tonight. I can go for a few more minutes, I guess.”

Tommy settled back in his bed triumphantly, as Uncle Dan continued his tale.

Danny found himself in the lobby of the building. He had lived in such a building before moving to his new house, but this one was in much worse shape. Two empty elevator shafts, each with a single wooden board propped diagonally over its yawning mouth, were located directly across the lobby from the busted doorway. Strips of peeling paint hung from the water-stained walls, and a ghostly film of dust and crushed tiles covered the floor. Staircases, to the right and left of the elevators, led upward into the unknown gloom. Both were boarded up halfway up the first flight, with no indication that they had been recently used. The overall air of neglect and abandonment made Danny shiver, as he realized that one day, the building that he had called home until recently would probably end up looking very much like this.

The dust was noticeably disturbed on the right-hand side of the lobby, and upon closer examination, Danny detected some footprints leading up to a small landing that was located a short way up the right-side staircase. He followed the footprints up to the landing and noticed that they continued down a neglected hallway that was even more depressing than the lobby. Half-open apartment doorways lined each side of the hall, each revealing the sad remains of what was once some family's living space. Some of the doors were jammed shut, as if daring Danny to find out what was behind them. The footprints petered out most of the way down the hall, in front of one of the closed doors.

The door was locked, of course, but Danny just punched it open and entered into the living room of the abandoned apartment. The room appeared empty in the dim light that filtered in through the boarded up windows. Where had those two men gone? They could not have just disappeared...

Danny yelped in surprise as his next step was into thin air. He had not noticed the huge hole that had been cut out of the middle of the floor, and he tumbled helplessly into the dark before remembering that he knew how to fly. Halting his descent with a simple thought, Danny hovered in the space between floors. There was a set of rough wooden stairs set into the floorboards of the room above, but it was all the way to one side of the room and easy to miss in the half-darkness. Anyone unfamiliar with the setup would almost certainly have plunged straight through to the basement of the building, which was probably the point.

A bit spooked out by all this, Danny paused for a minute to calm down. Bullets could not hurt him, and he had made sure to drink plenty of pickle juice - he would not run out this time. What was the worst that could happen to him? Danny took some deep breaths and made the decision to continue on.

He floated downwards until he reached the basement floor. A few feet in front of him was the most massive door he had ever seen. Danny had seen a similar door once before, when his father had taken him to work. They had gone to one of the branches of the bank his father was employed at, and the manager had opened the vault where they kept their extra cash and let Danny hold a bunch of $100 bill packs.

"Enjoy, it, Danny," his father had told him. "It's not often you get to hold fifty thousand dollars in your hands, you know."

The door in front of him now was much bigger than the one at the bank, and seemed thicker as well. It was light grey in color, made of solid metal, and looked tough enough to stop an M-1 tank. It was very out of place in the basement of a supposedly abandoned building, though, and it was fairly obvious that its job was to keep out unwanted visitors. Like him.

Was he strong enough to get through this?

Only one way to find out.

Danny drew back his fist, and then slammed it directly into the center of the door.

Several minutes earlier, Frankie and Little John had stood in front of the door to "The Vault," as their regional headquarters was known, and had waited to be buzzed in. After their identity had been verified via the camera mounted over the door, the massive entranceway had swung open. They had proceeded straight to the front of the room, where an enormous man was sitting behind a crude metal table. The door swung back into place behind them with a heavy metallic thud.

The underground hideout was located in the basement of the abandoned building, which had been made into a "safe house" for the Mafia's Brooklyn operatives. All cash extorted from local shopkeepers was delivered, sorted and counted here, along with money collected from drug sales, gambling and other criminal activities. Mafia-controlled drug dealers picked up their supplies from this location as well, before heading out into the streets to sell their deadly merchandise. The large room was bustling with activity. Tough-looking men were sitting at tables along one side of the room, some counting and stacking piles of money, others assembling various weapons and loading ammunition. Cubicles had been set up along the other side of the room, in which members of the drug distribution crew were measuring out various powders and pills into bags for the distributors. The center of the room was kept clear and clean, giving the man behind the table a better view of the whole operation, which was just the way he liked it.

Frankie respectfully placed a sack full of cash in front of the huge figure, who was smoking a fat cigar while running piles of money through a money-counting machine. "Solid week, Mugsy. That old man getting shot last week actually worked out good for us."

The man behind the table raised a thick eyebrow, grunted, and ran more bills through his machine.

"Yeah, boss," spoke up Little John. "All the other store

owners got scared, and they all paid up on time this week."

Mugsy grunted again. "Maybe it was a good week, maybe it wasn't. The cops get nervous when someone gets shot. We don't need the attention. Make sure it don't happen again."

CLAAANNNG!

The room fell silent. All eyes shifted to the door of the Vault, which suddenly had a fist-sized dent in it.

Mugsy glanced up at Frankie, casually drawing a pistol from his belt. "You guys made sure you weren't followed?"

"Yeah, sure, boss!" answered Frankie, eyeing the door worriedly. He took several steps backward, as did Little John.

"Who's got door duty?" barked Mugsy.

"Uh, m-me, Boss," answered a heavily tattooed and very terrified man standing near one of the weapon assembly tables. "We weren't expecting anybody after Frankie and Little John, so I uh, took a little break…"

WHAMM!

A much stronger blow shook the whole room. The door buckled inward and came partially off its hinges. Tiles and dust rained down from the ceiling.

Startled yells and shouts filled the room. Tables were knocked over as men reached for their weapons. Mugsy studied the partially destroyed door for a moment, then put down his handgun and grabbed an AK-47 automatic weapon from underneath the table.

Little John was shaking in his shoes. "Wh-what do you

think that is? A rh-rhinocerator?"

"I have a strong feeling we're about to find out," growled Mugsy, aiming the machine gun at the doorway.

With a deafening boom, the heavy door was ripped completely from the wall, skidded across nearly the entire length of the basement, and came to a halt in a shower of sparks, right in front of the table where Mugsy sat.

The clacking of safeties being flicked off multiple weapons echoed around the room. All the men trained their guns on the now open doorway, several of them sweating nervously. The men in the room had all been hardened by combat of one kind or another, but none of them had faced this particular situation before, and their imaginations were running wild.

What could it be? What had the power to bash through such a strong barrier so easily? Some new police robot? Maybe a top-secret government project?

The last thing any of them expected was a young boy of about eleven in wrinkled green clothes, who strolled into the room as carefree as if he were going for a walk in the park.

The men looked at each other in confusion. Several of them began to lower their weapons, not understanding the threat facing them. Mugsy, however, although he certainly did not look it, was a very intelligent man. His boss had been very unhappy with the results of yesterday's attempted bank robbery, and Mugsy had gotten quite an earful about how the crew had been unable to handle a simple kid who got in the way. If this was that kid, there was nothing simple about him. Well, he was not going to make the mistake of letting the Big Man down. He would put this little punk in his place.

Mugsy pointed at Danny. "Blast him! Shoot the kid!

NOW!!"

The men knew better than to question Mugsy's orders. Some of them may have felt some remorse at having to kill a child. That was part of the business, though. Too bad for the kid.

The piercing roar of machine gun fire filled the room. Danny instinctively raised his arms over his face as more than a hundred bullets impacted all over his body. These bullets were higher-caliber than the ones used during the bank robbery, but to Danny they felt like nothing more than gentle raindrops. After a few seconds, he relaxed his arms so that he could see what he was up against.

The view was actually quite spectacular. The bullets, traveling at nearly a thousand miles per hour, caused sizable sparks as they smashed into him, flattened and bounced away, and there were lots of bullets. It was like being at the core of a fireworks explosion. His new green suit was holding up just fine, too. Not even scratched, despite the heavy fire he was taking.

Danny scanned the room through the spark show until his eyes lit upon Frankie and Little John. They were standing with some huge person by a table full of cash, and all three were shooting at him. Danny immediately headed in their direction. Gunfire continued to pour at him from all sides, as Mugsy's men could not comprehend that their shots were having no effect.

Mugsy emptied his magazine, and, just as he had feared, the kid kept on coming. He reached under his table yet again, this time for a little something he had saved for special occasions. This was definitely such an occasion.

Two of Mugsy's men finally got it through their heads that their guns were not doing the job. One grabbed a crowbar, the other put on a set of brass knuckles. They jumped over the table they had been crouching behind and charged at Danny.

Why they thought this would do them any good is something that can never be answered, because they had about ten seconds left to live.

Mugsy seized the handle of a rectangular metal case, set it down on the table and flipped it open. Set into the box's white styrofoam lining was a rocket-propelled grenade launcher and one high-explosive anti-tank (HEAT) warhead. Mugsy moved quickly to attach the warhead to the launcher. The weapon was meant to stop a battle tank, not a little kid. However, he had no choice if he wanted to avoid capture. He swung the assembled weapon smoothly over his shoulder and aimed it right at Danny's chest.

The two men attacked Danny, one clanging his crowbar off Danny's head, the other punching him in the back with the brass knuckles. The one who punched him broke three fingers, while the crowbar guy sprained his elbow. Neither man would be in pain for very long.

Mugsy noticed the two men just as his finger tightened on the trigger. He hesitated briefly, but he could not pass up the shot. Their bad luck.

WHUSSSHHH!

The RPG streaked across the room and hit Danny dead center.

It immediately became apparent to Mugsy that the high-explosive rocket was not the ideal weapon to use in an enclosed space. The violent detonation and shock wave caused a partial collapse of the ceiling and knocked most of Mugsy's henchmen off their feet. Heavy smoke quickly filled the room. Cash and other flammable objects began to catch fire, and secondary explosions from loose ammunition added to the general chaos. Mugsy, coughing heavily, staggered across the room toward the open vault door, Frankie and Little John following behind him.

Danny had been busy with his two attackers and had not even seen the grenade until it was right on top of him. He felt it impact on his chest, followed by a flash of light and a loud bang. While the explosion did not hurt him, it did take Danny by surprise, causing him to step backwards and fall over the man with the brass knuckles, or what was left of him, anyway. Danny, on his hands and knees, found himself face to face with a dead person, the first one he had ever seen. The person's shirt had been mostly burnt away, and there was blood, lots of blood, and…oh, yuck. Danny turned away, retching and nauseous, only to behold the burnt remains of the man with the crowbar.

Danny closed his eyes and swallowed hard, trying to stay in control. He really did not want to throw up. Besides hating the way it felt, expelling the contents of his stomach, which included the pickle juice, might not be the best idea at this time. Danny remained on his knees for a few moments, eyes squeezed shut, trying to clear his head.

Many of Mugsy's men were getting to their feet and attempting to make their way through the smoke and fire out through the vault door. Some tried to gather up the cash and bags of drugs, now scattered all over the floor, but most just headed for the exit as fast as they could. Those that were able to, anyway. Danny could hear moans of pain and cries for help from others hurt in the explosion. He did not feel badly for them. No one told them to shoot a bomb at him, and he was sure that these guys had caused a lot of pain and suffering to others. Like poor Mr. Marty. Nope, he did not feel sorry for them one bit. Speaking of which…

Where were those men who shot Mr. Marty? He really wanted to make sure they ended up in jail. Danny peered through the smoke, which was beginning to thin a little. There was nobody left at the table at the end of the room, which meant that the men he was looking for had probably gone past him in the smoke. He also was curious about that huge man who had launched the missile at him. Who was that? Maybe he was their boss! It sure would be great if he could send him to jail, too. Danny turned and headed back toward the vault door as well.

There were many people on the stairs, gasping for breath and pushing each other out of the way to escape the smoking ruin that had been their hideout. Danny, who was not coughing in the slightest, marveled that the poor air quality was having absolutely no effect on his ability to breathe. He stood on tiptoes trying to find the men he was looking for, and then mentally smacked himself. Why was he acting like a regular kid? He could fly! Danny jumped into the air and floated up into the space between the basement and the first floor, searching the stairway running up the wall to his left. However, none of the men on the stairs were the ones he was interested in. They must have gone outside. He put on a burst of speed, shot through the hole in the floor above and zoomed out towards the front door of the building.

Frankie and Little John were one of the first ones out of the building, and had stumbled, coughing, into the bright sunshine. The first thing Little John noticed was that there were a lot of cars parked across the street. Usually the street was empty...oh no. The vehicles had sirens on top! Cops! He could not go back to jail. It was horrible in there. He was about to reach for the pistol he kept in a holster under his left arm, then realized that the police already had their weapons drawn, and they were aimed at him.

The shrill whine of a megaphone pierced the air.

"THIS IS CAPTAIN FAZIO OF THE NYPD. DROP YOUR WEAPONS AND GET DOWN ON THE FLOOR, HANDS BEHIND YOUR HEADS!"

Things did not look good for Frankie and Little John.

Until someone did something extremely stupid.

Captain Fazio's police cruiser had just pulled up in front of the address given to them by the 911 operator when a muffled thump from inside the building shook loose several bricks and window frames and sent them crashing to the sidewalk below. The captain, sitting in the passenger seat, shared a knowing glance with Officer Thompson, who had been driving. Both were Army veterans and instantly recognized the sound of a heavy weapon discharging indoors.

"Ok, Thompson. Let's set up a standard perimeter fifty feet from the entrance and hold position. No one goes near the building until I say so. I want clear lines of fire. That wasn't some little firecracker we just heard!"

"Right away, Captain!"

"As for you two," said Fazio, turning to Petersen and Bowman in the back seat, "you stay here. Do not, and I repeat, DO NOT," he emphasized, glaring at Petersen, "interfere with the ongoing police action." He grabbed the radio. "This is the Captain. I want all available units in the area to proceed to my location. I want the SWAT team here as well. All available units. On the double!"

Fazio got out of the car to direct his men. He turned back to Petersen as he headed off. "Remember. DON'T MOVE."

Mr. Petersen smiled thinly, waited approximately ten seconds after Captain Fazio left, then opened the door on his side of the cruiser and began to get out.

"Um, Mr. Petersen? The captain told us..."

"Let me show you how a real reporter works, sonny boy. We don't take orders from these clowns," Mr. Petersen cracked disdainfully. "Nothing but a bunch of grown men playing cops and robbers." He took a portable microphone and recorder out of his jacket pocket and edged towards the barricade of police officers and vehicles that was beginning to form around the building entrance. "Be a man and grab your video camera too, son. Maybe there's some hope for you yet!"

Benjamin did not want to disobey police orders, but he didn't want to lose Mr. Petersen's trust in him, either. Petersen was the boss, after all, and Benjamin did need this job. He opened his door, took a hesitant step out, and turned on his camera. He could use the zoom lens from here.

Captain Fazio crouched next to Officer Thompson behind a police car parked directly across from the open doorway of the building. Tendrils of smoke began to drift out, and he could make out the sounds of shouting and screaming as well. Fazio pulled his revolver and focused on the entrance. Some big muscle-bound guy was laying face-down off to the side, and chunks of brick and loose pieces of wood littered the sidewalk in front of the opening. Debris from the explosion? Didn't make sense….then he noticed the heavy slab of wood in the middle of the street, which, from the looks of things, had recently been covering the doorway. Something, or someone, had ripped the thing right out of the front of the building. How…? Then the first of Mugsy's men began stumbling out, coughing and rubbing their eyes. The Captain's eyes lit up.

"Are those guys who I think they are?" asked Thompson excitedly.

"Incredible. Frankie and Little John Camanetti. We've been after them for years!" whispered Fazio.

"And look who's behind them! It's like, half the Mafia!

This must've been some major safe house or something!" Thompson could barely control himself.

"This could really be big," the Captain agreed. "Ok, let's play it by the book. We don't want to mess this up." He took a megaphone from the car and stood up.

"THIS IS CAPTAIN FAZIO OF THE NYPD. DROP YOUR WEAPONS AND LIE DOWN ON THE FLOOR, HANDS BEHIND YOUR HEADS! YOU HAVE THE RIGHT TO REMAIN SILENT..."

Fazio's well-trained officers aimed their weapons steadily at the men emerging from the building. The Captain could not believe his good fortune. One after another long-time resident of wanted lists throughout the tri-state area were dazedly raising their arms in surrender. A great victory over the criminal forces that plagued the city was in his grasp. Could it really be all because of some kid calling himself "Pickle Boy"? It seemed too good to be true...

Someone rushed past him and right through the police lines, directly toward Frankie and Little John.

"WHAT THE..." Fazio rasped.

Petersen held out his microphone in front of the two men who had emerged first from the building. "This is Mike Petersen reporting for Big Apple News. We have unconfirmed reports of suspicious activity occurring within this building. Do you men have any information about what happened inside? Is it true that the young man calling himself Pickle Boy was involved?"

Fazio's voice came roaring through the megaphone. "PETERSEN! STEP AWAY FROM THOSE MEN IMMEDIATELY!"

"Pickle Boy, huh?" Frankie smiled nervously and glanced back toward the smoking doorway behind him. "Tell you what, Mr. News Guy. I'll help you if you help me."

"And how can I help you?"

"Well, for starters, you can be our ticket out of here." He grabbed Mr. Petersen's arm, twisted it behind his back, and pressed a pistol against the side of the newsman's head. "I'm Frankie, and this here's Little John. You're gonna be a good boy now and do exactly as I say."

"What are you doing? Unhand me!" demanded Mr. Petersen. "Do you have any idea who I am?"

"I don't care who you are, Fancypants. But for now, me and Little John will call you Mr. Hostage." Frankie turned him around to face the police officers. "Back off or the news guy is history!" he snarled.

"Oh boy," exclaimed Officer Thompson.

Captain Fazio was completely disgusted at the turn of events. That idiot Petersen had just put the success of the whole operation, and possibly his stupid life, in jeopardy. The Captain, though, had very little choice at this point. Saving lives is what his department did. Although he did have a fleeting urge (quickly suppressed) to just let the mobsters shoot that miserable know-it-all.

"Order the men to lower their weapons, Thompson. We'd better call in the hostage negotiation team."

"Oh, BOY!" repeated Officer Thompson, pointing at the building entrance.

Danny shot through the front door of the apartment

building and stopped short in mid-air, taking in the scene in front of him. He was happily surprised to see all the police cars surrounding the building. They had actually responded to his 911 call! Hey, wait. Why weren't they arresting any of these people...? Oh. One of his two "buddies" was holding a gun to someone's head! Well, he could take care of that. But he would have to be careful. He did not want that man to get hurt. Maybe if he went really fast...

Captain Fazio gawked, open-mouthed, at where Officer Thompson was pointing. At the boy, hovering ten feet off the ground, as if it was a perfectly natural thing to do. Then the boy's image became a blur as it moved at incredible speed toward Frankie and his hostage.

Danny's plan had been to zoom up behind the man holding the gun and pluck it out of his hand from behind. Unfortunately, he underestimated the speed he was traveling at, and before he could stop himself, he barreled directly into Frankie's back. The force of the collision sent Frankie hurtling towards the line of police cruisers. Frankie had time for a short, high-pitched scream before his body splintered the windshield of Captain Fazio's cruiser and landed, bloody and unconscious, in the front passenger seat.

Mr. Petersen had been knocked to the ground as well, and while he was grateful that Frankie was no longer a threat, the rescue had been a bit clumsy. His suit pants had been ripped at both knees! Clowns, that's all they were. Still, he should probably make the effort to thank the officer responsible.

"P-p-please, don't h-hurt me!" someone whimpered nearby. Petersen looked up and saw Little John cowering in fear. The man's terrified gaze was on someone behind Petersen, and whoever he was looking at was causing this tough career criminal to tremble like a frightened child. "H-here, I'm putting down my gun. I give up. Please! Whatever you are, I'm really sorry!"

Little John dropped his gun, lay down on the sidewalk and began to sob. Two officers quickly swarmed in and handcuffed him, while others moved to arrest the rest of the men who continued to stream out of the building. None of them put up any resistance, as they all seemed to be in a state of shock from what they had just witnessed.

Petersen was taken aback. This must be some special officer, to inspire this kind of fear in these hardened Mafioso. Perhaps he would have him as a special guest on his news show. This officer's story would be sure to attract high ratings. He gathered himself to his feet, prepared his most professional smile, and turned to meet his savior, who turned out to be….

Officer Thompson, who was standing next to some kid wearing strange green clothing. Guess Thompson was tougher than he looked, thought Petersen.

"Thank you, Officer. Good job taking care of that piece of trash. Next time try not to knock me over, hmmm? This is an expensive suit, you know. Brooks Brothers."

Thompson shook his head. "What are you talking about? I didn't rescue you. You're lucky anyone did, after you pulled that ridiculous stunt. Against the Captain's direct orders, too. No, you can thank this boy, here, for that." Thompson gestured to Danny. "Hey, you must be the one who called in to 911. Pickle Boy, huh? Good to see you again. You do smell like pickles, you know."

Danny blushed. "I know, my friends told me." He turned to the newsman. He felt bad about knocking him down, but at least he did not appear to be hurt. "Uh, hi, mister. Um…Sorry about your pants. Are you ok?"

Petersen stood with his mouth agape, unable to speak for several seconds, as his mind processed what he had just been told. The *kid* had saved him? The one he thought was a big phony?

"Wait," he finally sputtered, pointing at Danny. "You...you? You did all this?" he asked, waving his hands at the scene around him.

"That he did," exclaimed Captain Fazio, who had just come from pulling Frankie out of his car. He clapped Danny on the back. "Ow!" he winced, staring at his hand. "What are you made of, boy? Cement?" He picked up his megaphone and barked out orders to some cops near the building entrance. "Michaels! Walton! Take a team inside. Let me know what's in there. I don't want us to miss anything. And you," said the Captain, pointing at Petersen, "are not going to be getting near one of my crime scenes ever again. That little show you just put on was completely irresponsible!"

The captain turned back to Danny. "Son, I don't know who you are, or how you're doing it, but you just helped us grab a boatload of bad boys that we've been trying to catch for a long time!"

"Uh, no problem," Danny said sheepishly. "Um, you're going to put these guys in jail, right? They're bad people. Two of them shot someone I know."

"Absolutely, son. We're going to lock 'em all up, and there they'll stay. Well, at least until they get some fancy lawyers. But you don't worry about that. You did real good."

Mr. Petersen's mind was in turmoil. It was not a hoax. The kid was legitimate! Didn't matter. He was still in the right. And everyone needed to know that.

"Wait, wait. Hold on there, Captain. You're congratulating this kid?"

The Captain was becoming ever more annoyed at Petersen. "Why not? He helped us, big time! Unlike some other people who are just full of hot air and get in the way," he added sarcastically. Thompson and some of the nearby police officers chuckled. "Most importantly, no one got hurt! None of my guys, anyway. What more can you ask?"

Mr. Petersen snorted. "Oh, so now your little Pickle Boy is going to be doing all your dirty work for you? You think it is wise for little children to aid in police activities? Has he been properly trained for this? What happens when he makes mistakes? And he will make mistakes. Assuming he's human, of course." He suddenly turned on Danny. "What exactly are you, kid? Are you some angel from heaven?" he asked, waving his hands exaggeratedly to mimic wings. "Or just some illegal science experiment? Maybe a kind of robot?"

Captain Fazio had just about enough of the obnoxious newsman. "Lay off him, Petersen. He's just a kid. A kid you probably owe your life to!"

This Mr. Petersen was beginning to make Danny feel uneasy. He did not understand why the man seemed to hate him. Didn't he just rescue this guy? Maybe those pants were just really expensive. Anyway, it was getting late, and his mother was probably beginning to worry about him. "Um, is it ok if I go now?" he asked Captain Fazio. "I gotta get home already."

"Sure, kid. We just need to…" Suddenly a look of concern crossed the captain's face, and he grabbed Danny's arm. Danny had not noticed before, but the sleeve of his green suit had several dark red blotches on it. "Son, is that blood on your clothes? Are you hurt somewhere?"

"I…I don't think so…"

Fazio's radio squawked. "Captain, it's Michaels. You're

not going to believe what's down here. There's cash, weapons, drugs, you name it. And we got some bodies, too. Fresh."

"How fresh?" inquired the captain.

"Five minutes ago. And it's messy. Looks like they got hit with some kind of explosive."

Petersen's ears perked up. He frantically looked around for Benjamin, and spotting him near Fazio's cruiser, motioned him over. "Start recording on my signal," he whispered.

Fazio's demeanor instantly became strictly business as he refocused on Danny. "Maybe you should tell us exactly what happened in there, son."

Behind him, Petersen motioned to Benjamin.

Danny shrugged. "Well, I went in there looking for the men who shot Mr., uh, a friend of mine, and they hit me with some kind of bomb, I think. Some people were close to me when it exploded, and, well..."

"Mike Petersen here for Big Apple News. I am standing with the boy whom all of New York is buzzing about, or "Pickle Boy", as he is calling himself. So, Pickle Boy, is it true that you killed some people in your latest effort to assist the New York Police Department?"

"Thompson, get that idiot out of here!" yelled Fazio angrily.

"I didn't kill anyone!" answered Danny hotly. "They tried to kill me!"

"Then whose blood is that on your shirt?" shouted Petersen, as several police officers hustled him away. "WHOSE

BLOOD?"

"I…that's…"

"Don't say another word, son," advised Fazio. "He's just trying to rattle you. We'll sort out the facts. You'd better come down to the station, though."

"I can't. I really have to go home."

"This isn't a game of cops and robbers, son. There are dead men in there and we have to conduct an investigation." Fazio softened his expression slightly and crouched down to speak to Danny at eye level. "Listen, kid. I know you're just trying to help. And we do appreciate your assistance today in capturing all these wanted men. But you can't just go off and do whatever you feel like doing, and leave the mess for us to clean up. There are rules to this kind of thing, you know. Laws and regulations that have to be followed, for the good of everyone."

Danny shifted his feet nervously. "I told you what happened. Those men must have been near me when the bomb exploded. I…I'm sorry. I really have to go." He turned away from the captain and jumped into the air, cleared the roof of the apartment building, and sped off. He did not even bother trying to figure out which direction to go in. As long as it was away. Far away.

Petersen was grinning madly. "You got all that, right, Benjy-boy? Oh-h yes, I've got him right where I want him. The little snot. When I'm through with him, he'll never want to show his face, and those ridiculous clothes of his, in public. Ever again! Ha HAH!"

Benjamin had indeed captured everything on film, and he knew it would be easy for his boss to make this Pickle Boy look very bad. It might even get the poor kid arrested. He just could not figure it out, though. He had to ask.

"But Mr. Petersen. He saved your life! Why are you being so hard on him?"

Mr. Petersen snorted. "You have a lot to learn about this business, sonny. A lot to learn. But I'll explain rule number one to you right now. If someone makes me look like a fool, I'm gonna bury them. I'll make them wish they were never born."

A Big Apple news van showed up shortly thereafter to take them back to the station. Petersen barked out commands all the way back like some self-important general. Benjamin watched unhappily as the technicians edited his footage. He cringed as, per Petersen's orders, the section where Pickle Boy saved Mr. Petersen from the gunman was cut out. The poor boy. He had just been trying to help. Now Petersen would take him apart, and his camerawork would be the source of all the damage. Benjamin was not very happy with the direction his new career was headed.

There was more than one way out of the basement hideout, of course. Only a fool would leave himself a single method of escape, and Mugsy was no fool. While the cops, and that blasted kid, were busy with everyone else, he had calmly retreated to the rear of the underground room, keeping low so as avoid breathing too much smoke. He had moved aside an old closet to reveal a small wooden door, which he had opened with a key that had never needed to be used before. A narrow set of stairs led upward and out into a small courtyard at the back of the building.

Mugsy reached the top step and turned around. Smoke billowed up the stairs behind him, and....what was that? An object of some sort, fluttering up the stairs…Just a bird. It was flying crookedly, as if it was hurt. Only one of its wings was flapping as the bird struggled to gain altitude. Probably injured when the rocket went off…hey, that was strange. The bird appeared to be trailing smoke, as if something inside it were on fire. That made no sense. Well he had more important things to worry about.

The concrete-covered area behind the apartment building contained the remains of an old metal jungle gym and a rusty swing set, sadly waiting for children who had moved away long ago. Beyond them was a low fence, which Mugsy hopped over with some effort. An unhurried jog down the block got him to his emergency getaway, an unremarkable ten year old sedan kept full of gas at all times, just in case.

Mr. Simonelli would rant and rave when he found out what had happened at the Vault. Millions of dollars worth of cash and merchandise had been lost. All because of that rotten kid. The Big Boss would get even, eventually. He always did. That's how he became the Big Boss. He was very good at removing obstacles. Everyone knew that Mr. Simonelli's enemies either died violently or disappeared without a trace. Mugsy was sure that this kid would end up the same way.

He actually admired the kid a little. It took some guts, busting into the Vault like that. Too bad. Mr. Simonelli always won. That's just the way things were.

Dr. Picolo sat on the floor of his cell that afternoon, nursing the cuts and bruises that covered his body from the previous day's beatings. Mr. Simonelli's rare appearances in his cell were never pleasant ones, and the visit on Wednesday had been no exception. The Mafia chief had again demanded the whereabouts of the secret formula, and he had once again refused. The abuse had begun shortly thereafter. Well, he had not broken for the last twenty years, and he certainly would not now. Simonelli could never be allowed to get his hands on the formula. For the sake of human civilization, Picolo suffered whatever tortures Simonelli's men dreamed up. No one was even aware of his sacrifice. But now there was some hope. Just maybe, this boy would one day be able to put an end to all this.

Simonelli had not possessed his usual cool demeanor during his brief but violent visit, and had seemed quite agitated by something that had happened in the outside world. Curious to find out what had so upset the tough Mafia boss, Picolo had decided to risk viewing the latest reports from his pet pigeon. Fortunately, he had smuggled the bird into his cell before Simonelli's arrival. He had lain on his thin mattress, unable to sleep anyway from the pain of the beatings, until approximately three o'clock on Thursday morning, a time during which the guards tended to be either half-asleep or staring mindlessly at some late-night TV infomercial. Cupping his pet pigeon in his hands, he had turned his body towards his cell wall, shielding the bird from the guards' view. He had flipped out the video screen wing and observed the account of the foiled bank robbery with mounting amazement.

There was no doubt that the child had found the formula, but the results the boy was achieving were beyond anything Picolo had thought possible. Brain utilization in the subject must be over 80%! He had theorized that even 40% would be a remarkable breakthrough. He needed to have more data! The full extent of the boy's abilities had to be precisely determined. Perhaps, when he had a firmer grasp on what he was dealing with, he could even convey instructions to this exceptional young man through the pigeon. Some pointers, or maybe a little mental training. Right now, the boy was doing everything on his own. With his expert assistance, the possibilities were limitless!

He had decided then and there that he could not afford to stay on the sidelines any longer. He could not remain hidden away and not take responsibility for what he had created. Yes, he was wrong for letting loose his invention into the world, where it could be misused by men like Simonelli. He supposed that he should have destroyed it all when he had the chance. The reason he hadn't, at the time, was his hope that one day he would be able to use his life's work, the P3 formula, for the betterment of humanity.

Formula P3. He had started out with such good intentions, but for all the trouble his invention had caused, and could still cause, it would have been better if he had never discovered the unique ingredients that had made it possible. At least he had been fortunate enough to hide the stuff away before Simonelli realized that he had already completed it.

Of course, he had not been able to perfect the formula on the first, or even second, attempt. Formula P1 had been a disaster. Something had gone horribly wrong – to this day, he did not know exactly what his error had been. What he had produced was the exact opposite of what he had intended. The resulting black, gelatinous mass had acted as a sort of mental poison; even being in the same room with it had made him nauseous. Getting up close to it caused even more disturbing effects. He felt as if his brain were fighting *against* his body, instead of making it more productive. It was difficult, even painful, to make the simplest of movements. Even breathing had required extra exertion!

He understood immediately that this compound was very dangerous. If mass-produced by the wrong people, it could be formed into a weapon that could sicken, or even kill, millions! It had to be disposed of, and permanently. With great effort and concentration, and a considerable amount of pain, he managed to seal the evil material up in a heavy leaded-glass container, whereupon its harmful effects had been greatly reduced. He had then locked it up in his laboratory safe, put everything else on hold, and spent a month reassembling a rocket he had partially completed years earlier when researching his doctoral thesis. The rocket had been designed to be capable of escaping the Earth's gravity, and after some final tests, the black compound had been loaded aboard and launched into deep space, ensuring that no one would ever be harmed by his creation.

Formula P2 had been more successful, but after testing the deep red bubbly liquid with his instruments, he had uncovered a serious defect. Although the formula would meet his goals for vastly improving brain functions, the limited animal testing he had conducted had demonstrated that P2 would very likely cause anyone ingesting it to act in an aggressive and violent manner. Not exactly the miracle cure he was trying to produce. He had filled an eight-ounce sample bottle with the small amount he had created, marked it with a poison symbol so as not to confuse it with his other experiments, and put it on the side for later study. It took him another week to arrive at the correct combination of ingredients for the final P3 version of the formula.

Admittedly, there were still some issues, even with the final version. He did not think the boy had come across them yet, and Picolo could only hope that the boy would be able to control them, if and when these problems would manifest. He would have liked to have further perfected the formula, but an impatient Simonelli had been demanding results on an almost-daily basis. It was becoming harder and harder to stall him, and the formula had to be hidden before the mobster managed to get it in his clutches. Fortunately, he had remained on good terms with one of his childhood friends, who owned a house that was unoccupied. It came with the added benefit of an old-style nuclear fallout shelter in the basement. He arranged for some modifications to be made, a hidden entrance to be built, and then had transferred all of his work, even the sample bottle of P2 formula, to the hidden location in the dead of night. By the time Simonelli had finally lost patience and had shown up personally to collect the formula, every trace of it was long gone. At the Mafia man's command, Picolo had been dragged away and imprisoned. Regular beatings and torture had been among the methods used in their vain attempts to force him to reveal the location of his invention.

Picolo had suffered in obscurity, secure in the knowledge that P3 would remain hidden as long as he did not crack. But somehow, this young man had found the formula. Maybe his old friend's house had been sold to this boy's unsuspecting family, and the child had stumbled onto it through sheer luck. Who knew?

He had to accept the facts. P3 had been rediscovered, and it was much more powerful than he had anticipated. Now it was even more important that it not fall under Simonelli's control. He had to get involved, and for that, he needed to be as up-to-date as possible on what was happening in the outside world. At great risk, he had sent the pigeon out immediately, directly over the heads of the snoozing guards. These were desperate times, and desperate action had to be taken. Picolo trusted that it would find an open window somewhere to escape. He would wait for the pigeon to return, and do his best to hold out until then.

Joseph Picolo had managed to resist Simonelli for over twenty years. With all that had happened lately, though, he was afraid that Simonelli would be forced to do something reckless. Maybe some horrible new torture that would finally break him, or maybe a way to track the boy down and force him to reveal the formula's location. The Mafia boss would definitely be stepping up his efforts a few notches. For Picolo had learned over the years that Simonelli was not the only player in the effort to acquire the P3 formula. Not even the main player. Someone was pushing Simonelli to do his dirty work for him. Some unknown but powerful force. Picolo thought he might have an idea of what that force might be. If he was correct, there would be severe consequences for Simonelli if he failed to secure the formula's location. Severe consequences indeed.

"To be continued," said Uncle Dan.

"You always stop at the best part!" Tommy whined. "Please, Uncle Dan. At least tell me what you meant at the end. You said Mr. Simonelli would be in trouble if he didn't find the pickle juice. From who? I thought he was the one who was looking for it…so who else wants it? You said Mr. Simonelli was the boss!"

"Well, that's something I can't tell you yet, because Danny has no idea either. At this point, he doesn't even know about Mr. Simonelli. You'll find out all about this mysterious character at the same time Danny does."

Tommy mulled this over while Uncle Dan checked his cell phone. "Well, at least explain this to me, Uncle Dan. What's with this dude Mr. Petersen? Danny didn't do anything wrong. He didn't really kill anyone. He helped the police a lot! Why is Mr. Petersen trying so hard to make Pickle Boy look bad?"

"Good question, Tommy. All I can say is, some people get their kicks out of knocking others down. They'll do it to anyone, even to good men trying to help others, as long as it makes themselves look more important in the process."

"That's awful! Why would someone do that?"

"Don't be so surprised, Tommy. We all have a little of

that inside us. For instance, did you ever make fun of another kid because he looked or dressed a little differently from you and your friends?"

Tommy's face reddened noticeably. "Well, sometimes we mess around with this nerdy kid in our class. He stutters, too."

"That's what I'm talking about," said Uncle Dan. "You guys probably feel all big and important while you're making that kid's life miserable."

"I – I never thought of it that way."

Uncle Dan put his arm around Tommy. "Hey, I didn't mean to blast you there. Besides, kids make mistakes. The key is to learn from them and become a better man because of it."

"Imagine if Pickle Boy was like that," wondered Tommy. "You know, only caring about what's good for himself. That would be pretty scary."

"Well, he wasn't like that, but the people going after P3 sure are. Anyway, time to wrap things up. You need to go to sleep."

"Ok, ok, just one more thing. What about those other formulas? P1 and P2? What happens with those?"

"Well, P1 was shot off into space, as I said. And I mentioned P2 earlier in the story, if you think back. Hopefully, Danny will never have to deal with either of them. But you never know."

Uncle Dan checked his watch. "Goodnight, Tommy. I'll see you next week."

CHAPTER 8

ENEMIES REVEALED

"Uncle Dan, there's something I forgot to ask you about last time that you really need to tell me."

"What is it, Tommy?"

"You said something once about this story being in real life. Is this, like, a true story?"

Uncle Dan smiled mysteriously. "What do you think, Tommy?"

"No way it's true. People can't fly, or change their faces! Or not get hurt by bullets! That only happens in the movies or comic books!"

"But Tommy, people do fly. Every day. On airplanes. Nobody thought that was possible either, until around a hundred years ago. Who knows? A hundred years from now, people may be doing things that everyone considers impossible today."

Tommy was not entirely convinced. "Come on, Uncle Dan. If this stuff really happened, why didn't I ever hear about it before? I mean, there aren't any Pickle Boy movies or action figures, no video games, nothing! Wouldn't it at least be in my American History book? There's all this boring stuff in there instead!"

"Good question, Tommy. If it's all true, why doesn't anyone remember it? Well, what if something happened that made everyone forget the truth?"

"Whaa-at?" exclaimed Tommy incredulously. "How….how could that be possible?"

Uncle Dan's face turned serious for a moment and placed his hands on Tommy's shoulders. "Let's say something so terrible happened that Danny decided it would be better if no one had ever heard of him. That it would be too dangerous if the world remembered that there ever was a Pickle Boy."

"Whoa," said Tommy thoughtfully. "Danny can do that too? He can make people forget things? But what could have happened that would make Danny want everyone not to remember such an awesome thing as Pickle Boy?"

"Well," replied Uncle Dan, "he wasn't the one that did it. Erasing memories was not one of Danny's special abilities, but he *was* heavily involved in the decision that made it happen. And I wouldn't call it erasing… in fact," said Uncle Dan, with a mischievous twinkle in his eye, "what if I told you that all of the stories in those comic books and movies you just mentioned are, in actuality, just a replacement for the real thing?"

"What? I don't understand…."

Uncle Dan chuckled. "You're right. I'm getting a little, or rather a lot, ahead of myself. It's all part of a very complicated series of events, which I may not get up to for quite a while, and it's not directly connected to tonight's story. Why don't I just begin? I have a lot to tell you, because I'm going on vacation and won't be back for a month or so. I want to make sure that I have enough time to finish up. I'll try to answer more of your questions later, if there's time."

September 11, 2001. A day forever to be remembered as a day of great tragedy. Although from the standpoint of the terrorists and others who hated the United States of America and everything for which it stands, it was a great victory. With thousands dead and two great skyscrapers destroyed, the Americans had finally been hit where it hurt. But the Americans had stormed back, invading Afghanistan, killing many of the jihadist warriors and forcing the rest to flee in disarray. The Leader himself had almost been captured, escaping only at the last minute into a neighboring country. Then a new plan had been formulated. The next attack would kill hundreds, or even thousands, of times more than the strike at the Twin Towers did. The Americans would never be able to recover from such a blow, ushering in their ultimate defeat.

The plan had required great patience. There had been no major attacks on the American homeland since 9/11. The Leader wanted the Americans to think they were safe. The truth would catch them by surprise.

Eventually, the Leader decided to make the ultimate sacrifice to ensure the plan's success. He had leaked his secret location and let himself be captured and killed by the Americans in order to lull them into a false sense of security. However, his loyal followers faithfully carried on his teachings. The Americans would soon witness their ultimate nightmare visited upon them.

The best-trained, most loyal warriors had been sent to blend into the hustle and bustle of the target city. Over the years, they had become trusted citizens and had obtained jobs at key positions and locations. They would be ready to play their parts when the time came. A time that was fast approaching.

Danny eventually made his way homeward, unrolling the green suit from his body in mid-air as he got within sight of his house. The clothes promptly snapped into their closed-ball shape as soon as he got them off, except now there were some small red spots on the ball's surface. He would have to wash the blood out of his green suit before he used it again. If he ever used it again

Speeding up to avoid detection, Danny touched down in the driveway between 1313 and 1315 on East 13th Street, right next to the side door of his home. A passerby turned his head at the muffled thump of Danny's landing, but logically assumed that the plain-looking boy in ordinary clothes had been there all along.

Danny trudged up the stairs to his room while stuffing the green ball in his left pants pocket. A Prince Caprico doll that Miri had left on the landing at the top of stairs seemed to mock him as he passed by. He closed the door to his room behind him, flopped down on his bed and sighed. Once again he had tried to use the amazing stuff he found in his basement to help people, and once again things had gone wrong. The first time out, his clothes got shot full of holes, and he had been roughed up by Shia and his boys. This time, it was much more serious. People had died and he was being blamed, even though those men had been trying to kill him at the time. Maybe it was his fault somehow. If he would have just stayed away and let the police handle it…maybe that policeman was right after all. Maybe he was in over his head. Just because he had the power to do all those awesome things did not necessarily give him the right to use that power.

His churning thoughts turned to the pickle juice itself. For the first time, he wished he had never found it. His life had been so much simpler just a few days ago. Could he ever go back to being a regular kid again? Probably not. Even if he never drank one more drop of the juice, whomever it had been hidden from most certainly must have realized by now that it had been found. They would be looking for him. He would always have to be on guard. Tears began to form in Danny's eyes. Was this the kind of life he wanted?

It would be easier if he had someone to share his thoughts with. Someone who could help him with his problems. But who? As far as he knew, there was no one else on Earth like him. If he told his parents, they would probably just get all worried and call the police, and then everyone would find out who he was. That was definitely a huge no-no.

Danny's thoughts then turned to how all those barrels ended up in his basement. Whoever had made the pickle juice must have been very smart. Someone like that could definitely help him with his problems. But who knew how long the pickle juice had been down there? How could he possibly find out who had put it there....and then an idea came to him. It was an exceptionally good one (in his opinion), and he was especially proud of it since he thought of it with his regular, non juice-charged brain. He jumped out of bed and hurried downstairs to his mother's office.

The original plan was to set up Mrs. Green's home office for her speech therapy work in the basement of the new house. As with most home purchases, though, unexpected costs had eaten up too much of the Green's remaining savings for any further refurbishing. Mrs. Green had then decided to set up a temporary office in a narrow rectangular shaped storage room behind the kitchen, along the back wall of the house. Danny's father had plopped down a durable plastic folding table there, set up his wife's desktop computer, hooked up all the connections, and she was ready to go.

This computer was usually off-limits to Danny and Miri. They had their own computer to play with, but it had not been set up yet since the move. From the look of things, Miri had managed to get her mother to let her play her new Prince Caprico game on the office computer. Danny figured Miri must have whined away about how bored she was until his mother gave in. Typical little sister stuff.

Mrs. Green was sitting nearby at the kitchen table, busy scheduling her next day's appointments by phone. By the way his mother was concentrating, Danny was almost certain that she had been too busy to realize that he had come home later than usual. Well, at least one thing had gone right for him. Danny waited patiently until his mother finished her call, and managed to get her attention before she could start the next one.

"Mom, can you look up something on the Internet for me?"

"What do you want to look up?"

"I want to know who owned our house before we did."

Danny's mother raised her eyebrows. "Interesting question, Danny. Actually, I've been curious about that myself. I'd like to know who left the place such a wreck." She got up and went into her office. "Ok, Miri, scoot over for a second."

"But Mom-meee, I can't stop now! If I don't finish this level, I have to start all over again!"

"What if I do this?" said Danny, reaching over and hitting the ESC key. The word PAUSED appeared on the screen in pink cartoony letters. Miri's face turned just as pink as she fixed

Danny with a murderous glare.

Mrs. Green chuckled. "Ohhh-kay, Miri. Busted. Now let Mommy have her computer, please."

Miri grudgingly slid aside. Mrs. Green minimized the Prince Caprico game and opened her web browser.

"Prince Caprico!" shrieked Miri.

"Yeah, he's everywhere, isn't he," muttered Danny.

There it was on the Yahoo homepage. Sketchy accounts of Danny's afternoon adventures had already made it to the top of the news listings, right next to various pictures of him from the bank robbery the day before. All of the links used phrases like "unknown hero" or "mystery kid" to describe him. The top link was to Big Apple One, which once again promised full video coverage on the six o'clock news. Danny looked at the little clock in the lower right hand corner of the computer screen. It read 5:55.

Miri could barely contain herself. "Is he going to be on the news again, Mommy? Can we watch it?"

Mrs. Green stood up. "Remind me to do that search with you later, Danny. Let's go see what the latest is on this mystery boy."

"You mean Pickle Boy," said Danny, and immediately slapped his hand over his mouth. Miri raised her eyebrows a bit, but his mother was already on her way out of the room and was not particularly paying attention.

"I'm sorry, Danny," Mrs. Green said over her shoulder. "What did you say? Did you want some pickles? I think there are some in the fridge."

"Uh, never mind, Mom. You go on. I'll be there in a second."

Miri ran ahead to turn on the TV in the living room. Danny's father came home just as the news was about to begin. "I decided to leave early again," he explained as he put down his briefcase. "Everyone at the office did, too, even my boss! We heard there was more news about this kid, and…"

"Shhhh! It's starting!" said Mrs. Green and Miri together.

Once again, Danny slipped in behind everyone else, worried about what the news people would say about him.

The normally calm newscaster seemed a bit flustered as he began his report.

"GOOD EVENING. I'M STEVE MCLAIN WITH THE BIG APPLE ONE SIX O'CLOCK NEWS FOR THURSDAY, SEPTEMBER EIGHTH. OUR TOP STORY TONIGHT, ONCE AGAIN, IS ABOUT THE STILL UNIDENTIFIED BOY WHO SEEMS TO BE TRYING TO ASSIST THE NEW YORK POLICE DEPARTMENT. TODAY, THIS YOUNG MAN, WHO WE HAVE LEARNED GOES BY THE RATHER INTERESTING NAME OF "PICKLE BOY",

Miri whipped her head around and gawked at Danny. Danny noticed but refused to acknowledge her, keeping his eyes focused straight ahead on the screen.

"…ATTACKED A FORTIFIED BASE HIDDEN IN AN ABANDONED APARTMENT BUILDING, LEADING TO THE CAPTURE OF SEVERAL ALLEGED MEMBERS OF THE NEW YORK ORGANIZED CRIME UNDERGROUND, SOME OF WHOM WERE ON THE FBI'S MOST WANTED LIST. WHILE NO POLICE OFFICERS WERE INJURED DURING THE OPERATION, TWO MEN WHO HAD

ALLEGEDLY BEEN AT THE BASE WERE REPORTEDLY KILLED AS A RESULT OF PICKLE BOY'S ACTIONS. THE FOLLOWING IS AN EXCLUSIVE VIDEO SHOT BY BIG APPLE ONE REPORTERS AT THE SCENE. I MUST WARN YOU THAT SOME OF WHAT YOU ARE ABOUT TO SEE MAY BE CONSIDERED GRAPHIC AND NOT FOR THE FAINT OF HEART."

A short video clip played of Danny flying out of the smoking building. The words "Pickle Boy" (in quotation marks) appeared at the bottom of the screen. The next clip was of Little John seemingly begging for his life.

"P-p-please, don't h-hurt me!"

"H-here, I'm putting down my gun. I give up. Please! Whatever you are, I'm sorry!"

On screen, Little John dropped his gun and fell to the sidewalk, sobbing in fear. The camera then shifted to show a satisfied Pickle Boy looking on. It was obvious that the gangster was terrified of him. Danny's parents gasped at the image. Even Miri, the die-hard Prince Caprico fan, seemed troubled by what she was seeing.

Then it got worse. The news clip showed Mr. Petersen asking Pickle Boy if it was true that he killed anyone, Pickle Boy trying to deny it, then Mr. Petersen screaming "WHOSE BLOOD?" at which point the video ended.

Danny's father harrumphed and shook his head. Mrs. Green made some small worried noises in the back of her throat. Danny had to bite down on his bottom lip to stop himself from yelling at the TV. He could not believe how dangerous they were making Pickle Boy out to be.

"ALTHOUGH POLICE SOURCES ARE NOT

COMMENTING ON THE FATALITIES AT THIS TIME, CAPTAIN FAZIO OF THE 70TH PRECINCT WAS VISIBLY UPSET AT PICKLE BOY'S ACTIONS TODAY."

A video clip of Captain Fazio yelling, "Thompson, get that idiot out of here!" flashed on the screen.

Danny bit down hard enough to taste blood. The Captain said that to Petersen! Not to him! They were twisting everything around! Why were they being so unfair? What did he ever do to those news people?

The newscaster said some stuff about the "legendary" Mike Petersen returning to field reporting for this special historic event, and promised to keep everyone updated on further developments in the Pickle Boy story. Danny did not stick around to listen. With tears in his eyes, he ran out of the living room and back up the stairs, giving the Prince Caprico doll a violent kick as he passed.

After he had been sulking in his bed for a few minutes, his father came in and sat down next to him.

"Wanna talk it about it, son? I think I know how you feel."

"Really? What do you mean, Dad?" sniffled Danny.

"Well, when I was about your age, there was this pitcher on the Mets that we all thought was the greatest ever. It seemed that every game he appeared in, he pitched a shutout and struck out fifteen batters. Then one day they announced that he had been caught using illegal drugs. My friends and I couldn't believe it! We had all looked up to this guy, and he turned out to be a very messed-up individual with lots of issues. I remember how disappointed I was."

Mr. Green put an arm around his son. "You were probably all hyped up about that boy in the news. Pickle Boy, they're calling him. Hey, I was excited as well. It's incredible that there could be such a person in the world! And to think he's just a kid – probably about your age, too! Now they're saying all these bad things about him. That's why you're upset, right?"

Danny rested his head on his father's shoulder. "S-sort of. Yeah, I guess so." His father did not have it one hundred percent right, but it was close enough.

"Let me tell you something about the news. Lots of times they don't get their facts completely straight, or they change the facts just a little to make it agree with what they want to say. Especially that Petersen fellow. I remember when he used to be the news announcer. He was known for doing stuff like that."

Mr. Green scooped Danny onto his lap. Danny was a little too old for that kind of thing, but right now he did not mind.

"Don't let it get you down, Danny. I believe this Pickle Boy really is a good kid, and he's just trying to help. I also think that most people agree with what I just said. I can tell you personally that everyone at the office today was thrilled about the whole situation. In fact, that's all anyone talked about all day! That there's actually someone out there standing up against these…these animals who steal from people all the time. But besides all that, the truth has a way of coming out. No matter what Petersen tries to do, if Pickle Boy is truly innocent, and it wasn't his fault that those men were killed, it will all work out in the end. Don't give up on him. Ok?"

Despite not having a clue about what Danny had really gone through that day, Mr. Green had managed to say the perfect thing. His well-meaning words actually made quite an impression on Danny, and made him feel a whole lot better. Fathers sometimes know just what to say.

Mugsy pulled the emergency getaway car into the circular driveway of Mr. Simonelli's extravagant home in Staten Island, New York. He had driven straight from the scene of that afternoon's disaster to make his report in person, as the boss preferred. The vastness of the boss' mansion impressed him every time he visited. The driveway wound around an exotic fish-filled pool with a fountain in the center. The pool was surrounded by four massive marble pillars with stone benches filling the spaces between them. Those pillars were matched by even taller ones guarding the main entranceway of the mansion itself. The brick three-story main house extended from the entrance for several hundred feet in each direction. The front door was twenty feet high, made of imported polished white oak and topped by a huge picture window that went all the way up to the roof. An exquisite chandelier hung in the center of the front hall and was visible through the picture window. It was quite a sight when lit up, as it was this late afternoon.

Mugsy maneuvered his substantial body out of the car and stretched. The two men guarding the front door were eyeing the beat-up getaway car, which was a rather significant step down from the sleek Cadillac that Mugsy usually drove. The Caddy was still in Brooklyn, though, in a parking lot near the Vault. He would need to send someone to recover it, eventually. Right now, he had more important things on his mind.

The house guards smirked at each other as Mugsy made his way up the polished marble stairs. One of them eventually sauntered over to open the door for him. "Nice car, Mugsy," he cracked. "Haven't seen it yet. Present from your mother?"

"Shaddup, stupid. It's the getaway car. You know what that means. How's the boss? Did he hear about the Vault yet?"

The guard sobered up immediately. "Oh man, you were

at the Vault? We heard something happened there, but nobody knows nothing. The boss is going nuts. You better get in there."

Mugsy impatiently moved passed the guard and entered the mansion. He was greeted by the sight of one of Mr. Simonelli's less intelligent relatives, a rather dim-witted fellow known as Bugsy. Mugsy and Bugsy were similar in size, but differed in almost everything else. Unlike Mugsy, whose muscular bulk had been earned through weight lifting and exercise, Bugsy was an enormous ball of fat, and he moved with the grace of a drunken hippopotamus. He was also mostly useless. Bugsy would not come close to being on the top-ten list of people that you would ask to do anything of importance. It was common knowledge that Bugsy got to hang around the mansion only as a favor to the boss's mother, who was cousins with Bugsy's mother. Mugsy and the others tolerated him as best as they could to keep the boss happy, but it wasn't easy, especially considering Bugsy's annoyingly squeaky, high-pitched voice.

"Heyyyy, Mugsy, what's up?" Bugsy said, in his best trying-to-be-cool voice.

Mugsy tried his best not to show his disgust. "Uh, not much, Bugs. Where's the boss? I need to see him right away."

"Oh, I get it. You can't tell me about it. Hush hush. Nobody tells me nuttin'. Why is that?"

Mugsy's limit had been reached. He had gone through too much today to put up with this. "Bugsy!" he snapped. "This is important. I need to see him, NOW!"

Bugsy backed off. "Ok, ok, I'm just jokin' around. He's in the kitchen. Or maybe his office? Uh, or maybe…"

Mugsy had no more time to waste with this useless pile of

blabbering blubber. He would be nice and polite next time. Maybe. He raised his hand to cut off any more chatter from Bugsy and purposefully moved past him and down the ornate front hall. Rooms full of expensive furniture and artwork lined each side of the hallway, but they were all unoccupied. Then a long and loud string of very rude words blasted from the den area at the rear of the house. His stomach tightening, Mugsy headed in that direction. The boss was obviously not in a good mood. Mr. Simonelli did not handle disappointments very well.

Mugsy stopped at the den's arched entranceway. Mr. Simonelli was glaring at his 60-inch plasma TV, which was displaying the Big Apple One broadcast. The smoking shell of the Vault was visible in the background, behind some news guy with an annoying, know-it-all voice. Handcuffed men were shown being shoved into police cars. The boss' face was red with anger, a vein in his thick neck throbbing noticeably.

"Who the (#@!%) is that kid?" Simonelli roared. "If that's the same little (*&*#$!!) who messed up the bank job, I'll...Mugsy! There you are. Maybe you can tell me what the (&!#*!!) happened!"

Mugsy steadied himself and replied, "Yeah, boss. I think it's the same kid. He took down the Vault door like it was a paper bag. We did what we could. I even used the rocket launcher on him. Nothing worked!"

Mr. Simonelli fell silent for a while. Then he spoke, in the cold, even voice that sometimes made Mugsy wish he had a different job. "That miserable little (#%!*!#) just cost me about ten mil. Nobody does that to me. Nobody. I'll find out who he is, and I'll rip him apart!"

A soft yet insistent ringing sound emanated from Mr. Simonelli's private office off the den to the right. Mr. Simonelli paled noticeably. "Go on, Mugsy. Find out what you can about this kid. Use all our usual contacts. And take that fat slob cousin of mine with you. Get him out of my face. I – I have to take this call." Simonelli stumbled getting up from the couch, crossed over to his office and closed the door behind him.

Mugsy left. The way Mr. Simonelli sounded at the end troubled him. The boss had seemed shaken, almost frightened, as he went into his study. Who was calling on that phone that could cause such fear in a man as powerful as Mr. Simonelli? Mugsy tried to put it of his mind. He had enough to deal with already.

Mr. Simonelli sat down behind the hand-made executive desk at the rear of his office and reached for a compact dark grey phone, one that no one had ever seen him answer. This was because this phone had not been used for the last five years, and very rarely before that. When that phone rang, however, the Mafia boss, before whom even the toughest of men trembled, dropped everything he was doing to obey the Voice on the other end of the line. To not do so would be the equivalent of signing his own death sentence. One that would be carried out quickly, painfully and without mercy.

Hearing the Voice was an experience that shook him to the core. Years ago, he had a series of nightmares about this Voice, nightmares that still haunted him. In one of them, he had climbed a bleak, desolate mountain where thin, sickly gray grasses were the only signs of life, and heard the voice resonating from some dark cave whose floor was strewn with blood-streaked bones (animal? human?). In another horrible dream, the Voice had emanated from deep inside a long-deserted subway tunnel, the sound of it sending hundreds of rats screeching in all directions. It was not much better hearing it while awake. It was an impossibly deep Voice, one that projected power and absolute mastery. A Voice that demanded obedience. A Voice, that, above all, you would never want to be angry with you. The

Voice was definitely upset now.

"WHERE IS THE FORMULA?!?"

Simonelli's face went white. The hand holding the phone shook violently, and he fumbled it for a second or two before he was able to hold it properly again.

"I, uh, well, my men…"

"SILENCE, FOOL. IT IS OBVIOUS THAT YOU HAVE NOTHING FOR ME."

Mr. Simonelli whimpered in his expensive, specially made chair, fearing the worst.

"THE CHILD HAS HAD MORE SUCCESS LOCATING THE FORMULA THAN YOU HAVE, DESPITE YOUR YEARS OF EFFORTS. YOU... ARE... A... DISAPPOINTMENT."

An intense, piercing spike of pain erupted in the center of Mr. Simonelli's brain. The Mafia boss tumbled out of his chair in agony, clutching his head with one hand. He held on to the phone with the other hand, though. He dared not let go.

The pain lasted but a moment, yet the aftereffects left the mobster severely shaken. He crawled back into his seat to await the Voice's next pronouncement.

"YOU WILL TAKE WHATEVER

MEASURES ARE NECESSARY TO LOCATE THE FORMULA. THE BOY MUST NOT BE ALLOWED ANY FURTHER DEVELOPMENT. YOU CANNOT ALLOW HIM TO BECOME A THREAT TO ME!!! OBEY!!"

The line went dead.

Mr. Simonelli remained in his office, clutching his head and breathing hard. The previous boss had warned him about the Voice shortly before he died. No one knew who, or what, the Voice really was, only that its wishes could not be ignored. Twenty years earlier, the Voice had ordered the old boss to funnel money to some obscure scientist with some strange ideas about ways to improve brain function in sick people, and then to steal the results of the scientist's work once it had been completed. Mr. Simonelli, then one of the old boss' most trusted lieutenants, had been directly involved in the operation. When the scientist, Dr. Picolo, managed to hide his finished formula before it could be "collected", the previous boss had directed all of his top men, including Mr. Simonelli, to turn the city upside down and find it, but despite their best efforts, they had been unsuccessful. That boss had died for this failure. The Voice had contacted Mr. Simonelli soon after, once Simonelli had assumed control of all of the Mafia's activities in the New York area. He had been instructed to find the formula at all cost, even if it meant using torture to extract the formula's location from Dr. Picolo. But the doctor would not crack, and had remained a prisoner in a remote country estate that belonged to Mr. Simonelli's family.

The prisoner had originally been guarded by Mr. Simonelli's men, until the day the men in the dark grey uniforms arrived. They had identified themselves as the Soldiers of the

Voice, and they had informed Simonelli that they would be assuming responsibility for the prisoner from that moment onward. This had bothered Simonelli at first, but he had to admit that these men were true professionals. More professional than his own men, anyway. They did their job, keeping Picolo under round-the-clock surveillance, and made sure that the doctor stayed completely out of contact with the outside world.

So things had remained until recently. Now the Voice believed that the long-lost secret formula had been found. By this blasted Pickle Boy. The boy had to be stopped. Aside from the fact that this rotten kid had cost him more than ten million dollars so far, it had just been made clear to Simonelli that his very life was now in the balance. He simply had to find a way to break Picolo. Even if it meant killing him, he must learn the secret location of the formula.

The Mafia boss managed to compose himself, took out his cell phone and made a call.

"Mugsy. Change of plans. We're going to visit the doctor. Maybe you can help me pound some sense into him."

Benjamin was sitting on the floor of his small rented apartment later that night, watching a rebroadcast of Pickle Boy's humiliation on the ten o'clock news. He felt terrible. He blamed himself for the awful way Mr. Petersen had twisted the facts. Pickle Boy deserved a lot of credit for putting a big hurt on the Mafia, but instead, the story had turned into an attention-grabbing spectacle on how great Mr. Petersen was. There was still something he could do to fix it, though. Benjamin still had all of the original footage on his camcorder. Luckily, Mr. Petersen was just a little too old-fashioned to realize that television was no longer the best way to get information out to the public. However, he had to be careful if he still wanted to keep his job.

He had to make sure that what he was about to do could never be traced back to him. Covering his tracks should not be too difficult. There were plenty of anonymous websites on which he could post the video.

Within an hour, the original unedited footage of the day's action spread like a raging wildfire throughout the internet. People had been trying to get more information on the mysterious flying boy from New York ever since he had first appeared, and this was like throwing freshly cut up fish into a pool of hungry sharks. All-time records were set for "most viewed video". The millions of comments, posts and tweets that were generated were a mixture of wonder and outrage, and followed this general pattern:

Picklefan1: "Kool! He knocked that guy right thru the windshield!!"

BigApp: "Hey, look what a jerk that guy Petersen was – and Pickle Boy saved him!"

Truthy: "That cop was calling Petersen an idiot, not the kid!"

Picklegirl7: "OMG! OMG! He looks just like Prince Caprico! OMG!

Oldman80: "That youngster never should have been there. He has no idea what he's doing. Petersen's right!"

TUFFGUY: "That's stupid. Those Mafia goons deserved it. If that was me in the weird green suit, I would have killed more of them!"

Oldman80: "You shut yer mouth you ignorant fool!"

BigApp: "Petersen's a big old liar. Media bias!"

Picklefan1: "Pickle Boy RULES!11!"

Picklegirl7: "OMG!"

The strike team had their final meeting with the regional commander at dawn the following morning. As he surveyed the small group of eager young men, the commander reflected on how fitting it was that their mission would be carried out on a Friday, the holy day of the week. The team reviewed every step of the plan in great detail. Agents had been placed throughout the city to maximize the destruction about to be visited on their enemy. If all went as expected, the team members had just hours to live. This did not concern the three highly trained men of the strike team, however. They had been promised eternal heaven as a reward for their success. They were only too eager to complete their mission, which, if accomplished, would result in devastation never before witnessed in all of history.

The meeting came to an end. The strike team rose, straightened their suit jackets and ties, and exited their Brooklyn safe house, suitcases in hand. They blended smoothly with the stream of morning commuters as they entered the New York City subway system at the Newkirk Avenue station. Two police officers, positioned near the turnstiles to screen suspicious people and packages, barely glanced at the smiling well-dressed "businessmen" as they swiped their Metrocards and went on through. The men waited patiently for the Q train that would take them to midtown Manhattan, a few blocks from their target. The weather was perfect – sunny and not too hot - just as it had been on that glorious day ten years earlier. The early morning sun glinted off the metal rails of the tracks as their train approached. Everything was proceeding perfectly. G-d willing, the Americans would not notice anything unusual about them or their suitcases until it was too late.

CHAPTER 9

NIGHTMARE SCENARIO

By the time Danny woke up for school that Friday morning, the top story all over the internet, TV and radio was about how Big Apple One had mangled the original Pickle Boy story. In addition, important-sounding "experts" were offering conflicting opinions on the related topic that was being discussed across the city, throughout the United States, and across the rest of the world as well. Was someone like Pickle Boy a good thing, a welcome ally in the battle against crime and evil, or would his inexperience and irresponsibility just lead to more problems? Danny, though, had no knowledge of these new developments. He went to school that day thinking that the whole world hated him. Well, they did not hate him, plain old Danny Green. It was Pickle Boy who they were bashing. He could just hide as Danny Green for as long as he wanted to. Maybe he should just not be Pickle Boy anymore. Then they couldn't say all those mean things about him.

While that seemed like an easy and reasonable solution to his problem, Danny shoved a small bottle full of the green juice into one pants pocket and the ball of pickled clothing into the other. Just in case.

Danny trudged into the noisy schoolyard with his head down, past groups of boys excitedly discussing the latest news. Some kids grabbed at his arms, trying to get his attention, but he twisted away before realizing it was just his buddies, Joe and Sammy. Danny noticed that one of Joe's cheeks was slightly swollen and purplish.

"DANNY!" Sammy had to shout to be heard. "Can we talk to you for a few minutes?"

The three boys found a relatively quiet corner of the yard. Sammy began apologizing for something, while Joe glared angrily at Danny. Danny did not notice, as he was still in a funk. He was not really concentrating on what Sammy was saying either, until Joe cut Sammy off and snapped,

"What is WRONG with you, Danny?"

"Huh?"

"You heard me. You know, every kid in the whole world right now is wishing they could do the things that you can do. What right do you have to be so bummed out? Why are you walking around looking like the world is about to end?"

"Hey, back off, Joe," Danny shot back. "You don't know what it's like. That news guy made everyone think I'm some stupid kid who gets people killed. Why should I bother to try to help people if they're just going to say nasty things about me? Maybe this whole Pickle Boy thing is a dumb idea!"

Joe clapped his hands to his ears. "Tell me you didn't mean that, Danny. You can't mean that!"

Sammy hated to see his friends argue like this. "Hey,

guys, let's cool down. Danny, maybe people don't hate Pickle Boy as much as you think they do."

"That's not what I heard last night," Danny retorted. "Big Apple One nailed me pretty good!"

"Well, you obviously didn't check the news this morning. Someone posted a video on the internet that makes the Big Apple crew look like morons. It shows that the police called that news guy an idiot, not Pickle Boy!"

Danny's mood brightened considerably. "Really. Um, I-I didn't know that," he said thoughtfully.

"Uh-huh. And you should just listen to what everyone in the yard is saying. Everyone is going crazy about Pickle Boy! The way he busted up that hideout, and all those tough Mafia guys so afraid of him – it's beyond cool! It's AWESOME! We would have called to tell you about it, but, uh, Joe and I decided a couple of days ago that, well…"

"We didn't think we should talk on the phone about this stuff," added Joe, who had calmed down somewhat. "You know, us knowing your secret and all, and you never know who is listening on the phone lines."

"Yeah, I heard the CIA has a computer that can listen to every phone call in the world!" chimed in Sammy.

"No way!" exclaimed Danny. "That's impossible!"

"Impossible, huh? This, from a kid who can fly!" Joe retorted. "So, no talking on the phone, okay? And one more thing. I just can't believe you said that you didn't want to be Pickle Boy anymore. You can't do that. I – I need you to…I mean, uh, just… whatever." He put one hand on his swollen cheek and winced slightly. "You can't quit just because some wacko says some nasty things about you."

Danny saw Sammy raise an eyebrow out of the corner of his eye. It was certainly nice to hear that things were not as bad as he thought they were, but what was up with Joe? He did not usually stumble over his words like that. And what was that bruise on his face all about? Did Joe get into a fight? Maybe it was something he could help with. Joe might not be comfortable with him bringing it up in front of Sammy, though. He made a mental note to ask Joe about that later, in private.

"Okay, guys," said Danny. "I got it. I hear what you're saying. Still, neither of you have ever been ranked out on television. You can't blame me for bumming out a little."

The first bell rang, signaling five minutes to the start of classes, and the three boys began to make their way towards the school building. They were the exception, though, as most of the boys in the yard were too busy discussing the Pickle Boy story to have noticed the bell. Danny overheard snatches of what was being said as he walked by. He was encouraged that almost all the comments basically fell into one of two groups:

a. Pickle Boy was the absolute coolest thing that had ever happened in history;

b. The Big Apple News people were a bunch of old losers who didn't get it.

Even the name "Pickle Boy" was getting mostly positive reviews. Shia kept trying to make everyone listen to his story of how he and his gang had beaten up this kid that everyone thought was so great, and that anyone called Pickle Boy had to be a geek. But for the first time in a long time, no one was paying too much attention to the Big Three. The mere fact that a boy, just like one of them, had stood up to the Mafia goons seemed to inspire the idea that maybe they did not have to be so afraid of people like that. Maybe the bullies of the world did not have as much power as they used to. Not with Pickle Boy around.

Shia finally lost his patience and started shoving anyone who did not give his opinions the proper respect. Danny made sure to keep a safe distance away. At least this Pickle Boy stuff would keep Shia too busy to pay attention to the list of kids who had not paid up yet. A list that most probably consisted of only one name. His.

The teachers had some difficulty establishing control with all the excitement in the air. It was not until the third period that the sixth grade finally settled down. Everyone got more serious when the history teacher, an engaging man in his mid-forties named Mr. Zelmanowitz, began to discuss the significance of the following Sunday, the tenth anniversary of September 11, 2001. None of the boys were old enough to remember anything from that infamous day, and Mr. Zelmanowitz tried to convey the sense of horror and helplessness felt by those who witnessed the attacks first-hand. Danny's class watched, in hushed silence, the frightening video of the twin towers of the World Trade Center being hit by passenger planes and later collapsing. As the disaster unfolded, Danny's hands went almost instinctively to the juice in his pants pocket. He felt himself wishing he could somehow jump into the scene and help prevent the attacks. This, despite all the trouble he had gotten into whenever he had used the pickle juice! He tried not to dwell on it too much. There was nothing that he could do about it now, and hopefully, something like that would never happen again.

Benjamin did not know exactly what to expect when he got to work that morning, but he knew it would be messy. He was not wrong.

First, there was the cluster of news people conducting

interviews in front of the main offices of Big Apple One. Apparently, other news stations, not having any of their own Pickle Boy video footage, had decided to report on Big Apple's lousy handling of the story. Benjamin actually had to brush off two interview requests before ducking into the building.

Then there was the chaos in the newsroom. Mr. Petersen, red in the face and clutching the morning newspapers in his hands, was storming around the office bellowing out instructions, most of which were incomprehensible. Mr. Dekel and Mr. Stevens trailed anxiously behind him like frightened sheep. The staff mostly sat in their cubicles and tried to look busy, hoping to avoid Petersen's attention. Benjamin decided that this was an excellent strategy and decided to do the same.

He tried to sneak into his cubicle without being noticed, but did not have much luck. "YOU!" Mr. Petersen thundered from across the room, pointing a very angry finger directly at him. The noise level in the newsroom dropped to zero as everyone turned to stare at Benjamin. "INTO MY OFFICE, NOW!"

Benjamin felt everyone's eyes on his back as he made his way to the corner office. It was amazing how loud silence could sound. Bob sympathetically clapped him on the back as he passed by, which helped a little. Benjamin's stomach clenched up with tension as he followed Dekel and Stevens into Petersen's lair. Well, at least he had done the right thing. They could not take that away from him.

Benjamin sat down gingerly in the seat across from Mr. Petersen, who dropped heavily into his executive leather chair. Dekel and Stevens remained standing, flanking Petersen on either side. Benjamin had no doubt that Mr. Petersen was about to fire him for allowing the full video escape to the world and exposing Big Apple for manipulating the news. He had thought of a way out, though. He could claim that his camera had been stolen.

The thief had released the video. It was a lie of course, but he reasoned that it was ok to lie to a bunch of liars. Before he could open his mouth, though, Mr. Petersen began to speak, using a completely different tone of voice than Benjamin had expected.

"Sorry for yelling at you like that before, son. I'm in quite the mood this morning. And I'm sure you can understand why. One of our video technicians must have left the raw footage lying around, and it somehow ended up on the world wide internets."

Petersen sighed heavily, seemingly ignoring the bewildered look on Benjamin's face. "I try to inform the public in a responsible manner. Sometimes we have to leave some things out. Most people cannot be trusted to know the whole truth. And what is important for everyone to understand is that this boy is a menace. He cannot be worshipped like some sports superstar. He is a danger to society, and I know that you are with me on this, Benjamin. You were there yesterday when those men died. It was because of him."

Benjamin did not know what to think. Petersen was being nice to him! He had even used his full name! But why? Did Petersen really think that he agreed with him? Was he ever wrong. He could not forget the rotten way the man had treated a well-meaning kid who had probably saved his life. A boy who may very well decide not to bother helping anyone else if this was the reward he got for it. That sure would be a shame.

"There's going to be a lot of heat headed our way now," Petersen continued, "and I don't want you to be caught in the middle of it. I am placing you on a temporary assignment with the weather team for a while. On Fridays, they do a live weekend forecast from the observation deck of the Empire State Building. Why don't you tag along with them? That will keep you out of harm's way."

Benjamin was in wholehearted agreement with this suggestion. It was a fantastic idea for him to get away from the newsroom for a while. There would be less chance of suspicion falling on him that way.

"Um, ok, Mr. Petersen. Whatever you say. Empire State Building, here I come!"

Petersen turned to his executives after the rookie reporter left, with a drastically different expression from the one he wore with Benjamin. "Make sure that kid gets nowhere near anything related to Pickle Boy," he snarled. "Get the paperwork started on firing him. That… insect is probably the one who leaked the video. I want him out of here as soon as this little problem of ours is over with."

Stevens spoke up. "Why not just get rid of him now? Why wait?"

Petersen rolled his eyes. "Honestly, Stevens, do I have to spell out everything for you? If we sack him now, he'll go running around telling everyone what he thinks is the truth about this blasted Pickled Boy. We will keep him around, under our control, until we can convince everyone that we are right about this. We'll get rid of him when this hysteria has died down, and no one will care enough to pay any attention to what he says."

On the way into the city, the strike team had enjoyed a picturesque view of lower Manhattan as their train had briefly emerged from the underground tunnels to cross the Manhattan Bridge. The city skyline had been dramatically altered ten years earlier with the disappearance of the twin skyscrapers. What was planned for today would make that attack pale in comparison. If they were successful, there simply would be very little skyline to speak of at all.

Twenty minutes later, the men emerged from the 34th Street station on Sixth Avenue, also known as Avenue of the Americas. It was a few minutes before nine o'clock. The men strolled calmly through the heavy morning foot traffic, taking care not to draw any unwanted attention to themselves. They were hardly noticeable among the thousands of briefcase-carrying men and women hurrying to arrive at their jobs on time. The team made their way one block east and entered the ground floor of the tallest remaining building in New York. There was a nice café there, ironically a kosher one, and the men settled down to a tasty breakfast. They had some time, and would need their strength and concentration for the task ahead. No need to go hungry.

At about 10:00 AM, the strike team left the café and approached the already sizeable line of people waiting to access the Empire State Building's observation deck. Everyone wishing access to the observation deck was subject to security screening before boarding the elevators that would whisk them to the eighty-sixth floor. This would not be an obstacle for the strike team. The chief of security for the building, a man named Jarrad, had been placed in his position several years earlier for the sole purpose of letting these three men in on the morning of September 9, 2011. He had been notified just the previous evening that he would be fulfilling his mission the next day, and was, of course, completely unaware of the overall plan.

Jarrad spotted the three men in business attire entering the building. He had no idea who these men were or why they needed to avoid the security line. A number of years ago, a man had approached him outside the mosque after afternoon prayers with a generous job offer. Jarrad had been out of work at the time, and had jumped at the opportunity. The hours were decent, as was the salary, which was increased by ten thousand dollars a year in cash if he agreed to waive some people through security occasionally, no questions asked. And today was the day he was not supposed to ask questions. No big deal to him. These people probably were some VIPs who wanted a quick trip to the top. What was the harm?

He went to greet the three men. With a warm smile, Jarrad shook their hands and escorted them to the front of the line. Some of the other security personnel raised their eyebrows questioningly, but nobody made a move to stop them. Despite the complaints of the other tourists (some of whom had been waiting for over an hour), Jarrad moved his guests into the next available elevator and joined them on their ride upwards. He tried to make some small talk with the men, but they did not seem interested, so he fell silent. No problem. As long as he kept getting his ten grand.

When the elevator doors opened on the eighty-sixth floor, the men moved swiftly and surely to the southeast corner of the outside portion of the observation deck. As they deployed, the team leader marveled at how easily they were able to breach the Americans' defenses. The nonbelievers would soon pay dearly for their weaknesses.

The strike team members removed official-looking badges from their jacket pockets and clipped them to their lapels. Two of the men bent down to open the briefcases while the team leader stood in front of them to shield what they were doing from the eyes of the tourists and observation deck staff. The contents of the briefcases were extracted, and the men got to work. It was a very delicate and complicated task, but the men had trained for years for this very moment.

Several hours passed by. Curious tourists kept inquiring as to what they were assembling, and the team's two bomb technicians had to stop and smile politely as the team leader would explain in perfect English that they were constructing a machine that measured the pollution level and air quality in Manhattan. He would flash his forged Environmental Protection

Agency badge and mention that they were part of a government survey team. The tourists would nod approvingly, linger for a few maddening moments, and wander on. However, every time this happened, valuable seconds were wasted. In addition, some steps in the assembly were a bit troublesome and took longer than expected. The team leader remained calm. Their timetable had a certain margin for error, and they were still mostly on schedule. Besides, they had to wait for the weekly Friday weather team to arrive. Their live broadcasting equipment was an essential part of the plan.

The team leader mentally reviewed the final stages of the operation. Jarrad was not the only one that had been contacted the previous evening. Dozens of agents throughout the city had been given instructions, which were to be carried out simultaneously. At the appropriate time, the team leader would send a text message to their cell phones, and the chaos would begin. The agents had no knowledge of what they were about to become part of, of course. They all believed they would be participating in some kind of harmless demonstration against the policies of the American government. In actuality, the steps they would take would maximize the panic and destruction to take place that day. Some of them would probably die as a result of their actions, trapped in the city with the rest of the infidels. No matter. Their sacrifice would be rewarded in heaven, as would the strike team's. And their holy moment was quickly approaching.

The weather people arrived to do their live Friday broadcast a few minutes after two o'clock in the afternoon. The bomb assembly was completed a few minutes later, just as the weathermen finished setting up their video equipment. The team leader could feel it in his very being. Everything was coming together perfectly for this special moment.

The leader trembled slightly from excitement as he sent

the text message. The Americans would never be able to mount a response in time. Their plan had worked flawlessly. Nothing could stop them. Very soon now, they would be making history.

Within the next ten minutes, a series of traffic mishaps occurred throughout the city. There were few injuries and no deaths, but the effects on the city's traffic patterns were enormous, and on a scale never seen before.

An oil truck spilled fuel across the outbound and inbound upper level of the George Washington Bridge. The fuel caught fire, causing several vehicles to erupt in flames. Traffic on the lower level of the bridge was shut down as well, due to several multi-car collisions.

Minivans with trunks full of oily rags were driven into both ends of the Holland, Lincoln, Mid-Town and Brooklyn Battery tunnels. Their drivers stopped halfway through the tunnels, got out and ignited the rags, causing the vehicles to catch fire and fill the tunnels with smoke.

The Brooklyn, Manhattan, RFK and Williamsburg bridges experienced a rash of stalled vehicles whose drivers got out, tossed their keys over the side and into the ocean before simply walking away. Traffic came to a complete standstill.

All of the major mass-transit subway lines into and out of Manhattan experienced electrical problems or switching failures.

The end result was that an overwhelming majority of Manhattan's eight million daytime occupants were stuck in the city with almost no immediate avenues of escape, except on foot.

City officials could not believe what they were hearing as the reports began to come in. They kept on coming, an endless stream of nightmare traffic disasters. At One Police Plaza in downtown Manhattan, some of the veterans of the 9/11 attacks began to suspect that something was up, that this could not possibly all be a coincidence. Their worst fears were confirmed when a gasp went up from the officer who was monitoring the local TV station broadcasts, who immediately flipped all of the police station's televisions to the Big Apple One channel. Onscreen, a dark-haired man dressed in a business suit held a gun to a frightened woman's head. He smiled, revealing a mouth full of perfectly white teeth. Then he spoke words that New Yorkers, in the back of their minds, always feared might one day be spoken, in one form or another.

"GOOD AFTERNOON, AMERICANS. MY HOLY JIHAD TEAM IS AT THE TOP OF THE EMPIRE STATE BUILDING. WE ARE ARMED WITH A THERMONUCLEAR WEAPON THAT WILL OBLITERATE YOUR MOST IMPORTANT CITY. DO NOT TRY TO FLEE. THE EXITS TO YOUR CITY HAVE BEEN BLOCKED. ANY ATTEMPT TO ATTACK US WILL RESULT IN THE IMMEDIATE DETONATION OF THE WEAPON. THE CITY WILL DIE IN TWO HOURS UNLESS THE FOLLOWING DEMANDS ARE MET."

At about the same time, Danny was walking home from school with his friends. Overall, it had turned out to be a halfway decent day. Shia had been too busy to bother him for the money, and he was feeling more positive about the Pickle Boy thing, although he had basically decided to give it a break for a while anyway. The last few days had just been a little too exciting. He had discussed the situation with Sammy and Joe, who did not totally agree with his decision but understood that Danny wanted a little less drama in his life for a while. Then they had made Danny spill all the details of the raid on the Mafia hideout. The boys were so wrapped up in their conversation that they did not notice the increasing sounds of horrified gasps and crying all around them, as people heard the news of the terrorists and their nuclear weapon. Drivers pulled their vehicles to the side of the road as the information came in over their radios. There they remained in stunned silence, motors running, as they tried to absorb what they were hearing. People on the street gathered around those with better internet access on their phones, trying to make sense of the sketchy accounts being posted online. Others just stood motionless, eyes fixed northwards on the tall spike of the Empire State Building, waiting for the end of the world as they knew it.

Danny reached his block before he finally realized that not all was right with the world. Most of the neighbors were frantically packing up their cars as if they were going on a sudden trip. Kids were crying, parents were yelling, and everyone seemed…scared. He hurried up the stairs to his house and went inside, a little afraid of what he might find out.

Miri met him in the front hall, eyes red from crying. She tried to tell him something but could not get it out before bursting into tears.

"Danny! Is that you? Oh my G-d!" his mother screamed, hugging him really hard. Then she broke down crying as well.

Danny really did not like this. Something must be very, very wrong for his mother to act this way.

"What's going on, Mom?" he asked, with a lump in his throat.

His mother could not stop sobbing, and jabbed her finger at the TV screen.

"THIS IS STEVE MCLAIN WITH OUR CONTINUING COVERAGE OF THE TERRORIST SITUATION. FOR THOSE JUST JOINING US, JIHADI TERRORISTS

CLAIMING TO BE IN POSSESSION OF A NUCLEAR BOMB HAVE TAKEN CONTROL OF THE OBSERVATION DECK OF THE EMPIRE STATE BUILDING. THE TERRORISTS ARE THREATENING TO DETONATE THE BOMB IN APPROXIMATELY NINETY MINUTES UNLESS THE UNITED STATES WIRES ONE HUNDRED BILLION DOLLARS INTO JIHADI BANK ACCOUNTS, ISRAEL UNCONDITIONALLY SURRENDERS THE ENTIRE WEST BANK AND THE CITY OF JERUSALEM, AND ALL JIHADI PRISONERS HELD THROUGHOUT THE WORLD ARE RELEASED IMMEDIATELY. THEY ALSO ARE CLAIMING TO HAVE CAUSED THE TRAFFIC AND MASS TRANSIT DISPRUPTIONS THAT ARE MAKING EVACUATION EXTEREMLY DIFFICULT. THE MAYOR HAS URGED ALL CITIZENS TO REMAIN CALM, AS THE PRESIDENT HAS ASSURED HIM THAT HE WILL DO EVERYTHING IN HIS POWER TO PREVENT THE BOMB FROM BEING DETONATED. WE WILL CONTINUE TO CLOSELY MONITOR THE SITUATION AND PASS ALONG ANY UPDATES WE RECEIVE. G-D BLESS YOU ALL."

Danny went white as a ghost. This was…was…

He could not complete his thoughts. His mind went utterly blank with shock.

Mrs. Green finally got herself somewhat under control.

"Ok, kids," she said quietly. "Get some stuff and let's get in the car. We have to be as far away from that thing as possible." She was having a sickening flashback to 9/11, when papers from offices in the World Trade Center had been blown all over Brooklyn. This would be much worse. She did not want what would remain of her family to be covered with radioactive dust.

"WHAT ABOUT DADDY?" screamed Miri, tears

streaming down her face.

Danny's mother broke into a fresh bout of weeping, and it was difficult for her to speak for a few moments. "I…I tried to call him," she sniffled. "All the lines are jammed. I heard it's impossible to get out of Manhattan. We have to leave before we get stuck, too. We…we'll leave a note for Daddy...just in case..." and Mrs. Green burst into tears yet again.

Something inside Danny snapped.

"THEY ARE NOT GOING TO GET AWAY WITH THIS!" he suddenly blurted. "THEY ARE NOT GOING TO KILL DADDY, OR ANYONE ELSE!"

His mother and sister looked at him as if he was from another planet. Danny made a quick mental decision. This was no time for secrets. He turned to his mother.

"Mom, I've got to talk to you. In private."

His mother was too stunned to argue, and followed Danny into his room.

The President of the United States had been whisked away to a secure undisclosed location even before the first terrorist broadcast had ended. A videoconference link to the White House Situation Room allowed him to hold a virtual meeting with the Joint Chiefs of Staff, along with the Directors of the FBI, CIA, and NSA, key members of the House and Senate, and any other important official that could be rounded up on short notice.

"Gentlemen, time is short. What are our options?" the President demanded.

The generals of the Joint Chiefs looked at each other, then looked away. None of them could meet the President's gaze. The Directors of the government agencies were not being of much help, either. After some moments of uncomfortable silence, the NSA man cleared his throat and stood up to lay out the bad news.

"Mr. President, let me just confirm that it is highly probable that the terrorists actually do possess a nuclear weapon. We have some preliminary radiation readings from midtown Manhattan, and the results are consistent with a thermonuclear device. I repeat, thermonuclear."

Gasps were heard from around the table. They had not thought it possible that the terrorists could get their hands on one of those. That meant that they were most likely dealing with a hydrogen bomb, which could be hundreds of times more powerful than the atomic bombs used against Japan in World War II.

The NSA man continued. "Not only that, Mr. President, but the terrorists picked a perfect location as well. Perfect for them, unfortunately. We can't get close without them seeing us coming from miles away, and they will detonate if they suspect we are planning to attack them. Additionally, the placement of the bomb means that any detonation will be what is referred to as an airburst explosion, resulting in the maximum possible damage such a weapon can cause. We're talking about a good chunk of the city, from Grand Central Station to Times Square, being nothing more than a smoking hole in the ground. You can draw a circle around that hole stretching for miles in all directions, inside of which everything will be reduced to rubble. At least a million, probably more like two million, dead. And many more will die from radiation poisoning within the next twenty four hours, if we can't get the rest of the island evacuated."

"So what are you suggesting?" barked the President. "We

should simply surrender to these madmen?"

"I don't think we have a choice, sir," answered the NSA chief.

"Let me remind everyone what we're dealing with," the Director of the CIA chimed in. "These clowns believe they go straight to heaven if they die killing Americans. It's very likely that they'll blow up the city no matter what we agree to give them."

"What we need," intoned the President, "is some kind of miracle."

Danny locked the door behind his mother and moved far enough away from it so that Miri, who would surely be trying to listen at the keyhole, would have a hard time making out what he was about to reveal.

He took a deep breath and began, doing his best to keep it as short as possible. Millions of lives were at risk, but his mother had the right to know what he was going to try to do.

"Mom you know that Pickle Boy that everyone's been talking about?"

"Yes, Danny, but that's not important now."

"It is, Mom, because I'm him, and I have to go save Daddy and everyone else."

"What…Danny, please, not now. There's no time for this nonsense. Come, pack some stuff…"

Danny reached into his pocket, pulled out the bottle of

pickle juice, and downed the whole thing in two gulps. He then snapped open the wrinkled green clothing and jumped into it, face changing as he did so. Then he floated a few feet upwards and hovered.

Mrs. Green gawped at him for a few seconds, then, her voice rising to a shriek, exclaimed,

"How…where…but…where's Danny? WHAT DID YOU DO WITH HIM?"

"Mom. Mom! Relax. It's me. I can change my face so that no one recognizes me. And I can also fly, and I can't get hurt, I think. I'll explain everything when I get back. But I'd better go. I can't let those terrorists do this."

Mrs. Green massaged her temples. Danny's real face peeked through the visual mask for a second, and she rubbed her eyes again. Then she shook her head in resignation.

"Ok. Whatever. Terrorists are blowing up New York. My son can fly. This must be all a dream. More like a nightmare." She squeezed her eyes shut and pinched herself on the arm, waited a few seconds and reopened her eyes. Danny was still floating in front of her, trying his best to be patient.

"This isn't a dream?"

Danny shook his head.

Mrs. Green slumped in resignation. "I…I don't understand. When did this happen? How can you do all these things? Is it that juice or whatever that you just drank?"

"Mom, I'll explain everything when I get back, ok? I've got to get moving if I'm going to stop these guys."

"But why you? Why do you have to go? It's very dangerous! It's an atomic bomb!" Mrs. Green's voice began to rise again as she went on. "Let someone else handle this!"

Danny floated to the window and flipped it open.

"Who, Mom? There is no one else."

He was halfway outside when his mother spoke to him one final time.

"Danny?"

"Yes, Mom?"

"This really is happening, isn't it?"

"Yeah. I guess so."

His mother ran to him and hugged him, hard. For some reason, Danny could feel it more than the rocket that had slammed into him the day before.

"Please be careful, Danny. I love you. And I'm very proud of you for trying. But please…please make sure you come home."

"I will. I love you too, Mom. And I'll make sure Daddy gets home, also. Ok?"

His mother nodded, tears streaming. Danny felt himself tearing up as well.

"Uh, one more thing, Mom. Don't tell Miri."

With that, Danny was off.

Danny's real face was not at all as relaxed as the Pickle

Boy face he had projected to his mother. Inside, he was beginning to get very, very nervous about what he was about to attempt. He could not let his mother see it, though. She had enough to worry about as it was.

CHAPTER 10

EPIC CONFRONTATION

Benjamin could not understand how he kept getting into these situations. A week ago, he did not even have a job, and now he had already gotten involved in the two of the biggest stories of the twenty first century, perhaps of all time. Soon after he had arrived on the observation deck with the weather crew, he had volunteered to help set up the camera for the forecast. Then this nutball Jihadist terrorist had pulled out an AK-47 and forced Benjamin, who was holding the camera, to broadcast their demands to the public, or they would execute the weather girl. After that, the terrorists made him focus the camera on the digital clock attached to the bomb as its blood-red numbers counted down the remaining time to detonation. The clock currently displayed:

01:21:59

and he truly believed these psychos would actually set the thing off if the government didn't cave. Probably even if they did.

The Jihadists patrolled the rooftop with their machine guns, occasionally making threatening gestures at one of the terrified tourists, who had all been herded into one area of the deck and ordered to sit quietly. Every so often they would stop in front of Benjamin's camera and shout out something like "Death to America" or "alla akbar". They seemed to be enjoying themselves a little too much.

Benjamin could not see how any rescue attempt could be successful without the Jihadists setting off the bomb, as one of them was always within a few feet of the weapon. He also noticed that at all three of the terrorists kept flicking their eyes at the doors to the observation deck. Anyone coming from inside the building would be quickly spotted, and any helicopter attack would be detected from miles away. The situation seemed hopeless.

Then, for a moment, all three of the terrorists were facing away from Benjamin and the rest of the weather crew. One of the video technicians got up from the floor where he had been sitting and leaned casually against the wall near Benjamin.

"Hey, kid," the tech person muttered under his breath. "Where's that Pickle Boy you were hanging around with yesterday? We could sort of use him here, you know."

The blow seemed to come from out of nowhere. The stock of the machine gun slammed savagely into the side of the technician's head. The man collapsed to the ground, blood dripping from a nasty gash.

"SILENCE, INFIDEL!" screamed the Jihadist. "ANY MORE TALKING, I START SHOOTING!"

The terrorist then turned his malevolent gaze on the much shaken Benjamin and his camera, which was continuing to broadcast the crisis live to the whole world.

"PEOPLE OF NEW YORK. YOUR GOVERNMENT HAS NOT YET RESPONDED TO OUR GENEROUS OFFER.

YOU HAVE EIGHTY MINUTES BEFORE YOU ARE TURNED TO ASHES."

Things were really going downhill, thought Benjamin. Come to think of it, where was Pickle Boy?

Danny shot skywards out of his bedroom window and headed north, towards the spire of the Empire State Building. He felt even less sure of this whole idea than when he was speaking to his mother. But he really was the only one who could save his father. If he could find him, that is. Danny had a vague idea of where in Manhattan his father's office was, but his father was probably not even there anymore. He probably would be trying to escape the city along with everyone else. The only way to save him would be to take out the terrorists and their bomb. He would have to be very careful. Danny certainly did not want to be responsible for the city getting blown up.

As he flew over the streets of Brooklyn, Danny saw that the avenues were beginning to jam up with packed cars and minivans. Lots of people must have had the same idea that his mother did - that if the bomb went off in Manhattan, Brooklyn was going to get whacked, too. Some of the people still on foot noticed him and began pointing upwards.

"Hey, there's that Pickle Boy kid from the news!"

"Pickle Boy! Pickle Boy! Are you going after those terrorists?"

"Yeah! Go get 'em, Pickle Boy!"

Others began picking it up, and soon there was actual cheering going on. Danny could not believe it. They were all on his side! They liked him! He smiled and waved, sparking more cheers. But he had no more time to waste. With renewed determination, he zipped off towards Manhattan like a streak of green light, leaving the crowd screaming behind him.

Officer Thompson, who was doing his best to maintain some kind of order in the streets, watched as Danny disappeared into the distance. He had mixed feelings about this development. The boy was clearly not experienced enough to handle a crisis of this magnitude. Yet, with so little time to prepare an effective response, there really wasn't any better option. Or any other option at all, for that matter. He could only wish the kid luck. And pray that the boy, and the millions of others who were in grave danger, would survive the next seventy-five minutes.

The Empire State Building loomed larger and larger as he approached the East River, which separates Brooklyn from Manhattan. Once again, all sorts of doubts sprouted up into his mind like hungry weeds. What was he doing? He had no idea how to deal with this kind of thing. Then again, neither did anyone else. But he was just a kid, not some trained counterterrorist agent. What if he screwed it up? One little mistake, that's all, and his father, and the whole city…

No.

He shook his head as if to shake out the negative thoughts. If he was to have any chance at all, he could not be dwelling on what might happen if he failed. He had to concentrate completely on what he had to do. Once Danny started to focus, the pickle juice began to kick in. It cleared his mind, dampened down the distracting worries and fears, and helped him stay on point. Seconds later, he shot over the river and entered Manhattan proper.

Danny crossed above the FDR Drive at 34th Street and on

into the city at a height of about fifty feet. He flew over streets jammed with people, most of them trying to make their way towards one of the bridges leading out of Manhattan. Not many vehicles were operating, as there was no way for them to escape the city anyway, but the pedestrian walkways across the bridges were mostly passable. Streams of men and women were pouring out of office buildings and into the streets, many reliving either the original 9/11 event or the 2003 summer blackout, during which many of them had no choice but to escape the city on foot. Just as they had done then, the citizens of Manhattan were moving in surprisingly orderly fashion, in spite of the looming disaster. There was some panicking, but overall, New Yorkers were acquitting themselves rather well. Unfortunately, most of them would not be able to get far enough away to survive the bomb blast if it went off on schedule. Still, trying to escape was better than sitting around and doing nothing.

Danny slowed down a bit. Somewhere down there was his father. He felt an overpowering urge to just stop what he was doing and look around for him. He could fly him, and then his whole family, far, far away, where they would be safe. He paused for a moment over Third Avenue, considering.

"Hey, look! It's that pickle dude!" shouted a food delivery guy, who was having little success trying to navigate his bike through the crowd.

"Hey! Pickle Boy!" screamed a lawyer in a dark blue suit and yellow power tie. "Are you gonna do something about those terrorists or what?"

"Uh…." said Danny. "I'll try, I guess."

The people on the street looked at each other with raised eyebrows. "I'll try, I guess?" That was not what they were hoping to hear. A solid, bravely voiced "No problem, I'll take care of everything!" would have been much more reassuring.

Danny was just a boy, though, and he was more than a little scared himself.

Then a teenage girl yelled out something that somehow fixed it all.

"GO GET THOSE CREEPS, PICKLE BOY! KNOCK 'EM DEAD! TEAR 'EM APART!"

The crowd roared and hollered, cheering madly. Danny smiled broadly, waved, and shot towards his destination, mere blocks away.

He got it. Everyone was relying on him, yet they were also on his side. He could not just think about his own family. The whole city was his family now. And those horrible people were trying to kill them all. He could not allow that.

Danny arrived at the corner of Thirty Fourth Street and Fifth Avenue ten seconds later. The Empire State Building was surrounded by seemingly every police car in the city. The frustrated police officers could do little except mill around on the street outside. They were under strict orders not to enter the building. Nobody wanted to give the terrorists an excuse to set off the bomb.

Several of the officers spotted Danny. One of them grabbed a megaphone and shouted,

"Hey! Get down! You're not going anywhere, kid! Nobody goes near the Building!"

Danny hesitated. The police could not actually stop him, but he did not want to disobey the law, either. Then he saw a familiar face yank the megaphone away from the officer who had ordered him down.

"Pickle Boy! Please come down for a minute. We need to talk!"

Danny floated down and landed next to Captain Fazio. The policemen nearby backed away slightly and formed a circle around them. Some of them even drew their weapons, but Danny pretended not to notice.

"Lucky for me I happened to be in the city for a captain's meeting when this whole thing started, huh, kid?" Fazio rumbled. "Now I'm stuck here with everyone else. Good to see you again, boy."

"Uh, thanks, I guess. I really want to help."

Fazio bent down and put an arm around Danny, and, out of Danny's eyesight, motioned impatiently with his other arm for the idiots who had pulled their guns to re-holster them. Didn't they know that their weapons would not do much good, anyway?

"As far as I can tell, we have no workable options here," whispered Fazio into Danny's ear. "The good folks in Washington haven't given us anything worthwhile yet. We can't take them by surprise, and I am pretty sure that these murderers are gonna blow the blasted thing even if we give them everything they want. I saw what you did yesterday, what you can do. They won't be ready for you. You should be able to take them out before they realize what's happening. Just make sure you don't let them set off the bomb. That's the number one priority!"

"I got it. I got it," repeated Danny. "Take out the bad guys before they can set off the bomb."

"Good. Now go, before someone here decides they have a better idea."

Captain Fazio clapped Danny on the back for

encouragement. His confidence refueled once more, Danny launched himself up the side of the building. The upward gust of wind blew off the hats of all the nearby officers, except for Fazio, who calmly held his by the brim.

"Captain, I don't think that was a very good idea," remarked the officer whose megaphone Fazio had "borrowed".

Fazio harrumphed disgustedly. "It's a whole lot better than no idea, which is what we've had until now," he replied. "He really is our best, and only, hope." He raised his eyes skyward at the receding green dot zipping up the side of the building. "May G-d help us all."

This was by far the highest Danny had ever ascended in his brief flying career. At some point, roughly around the sixtieth floor, he took a quick look downward and almost threw up. Danny squeezed his eyes closed to control the queasiness and thought calming thoughts. He would not fall. He had plenty of pickle juice in his system. Nothing here could hurt him. It was the situation on the roof that he had to worry about. He opened his eyes again and resumed his journey upwards.

He finally reached the observation deck and grabbed on to the edge of the building with both hands, keeping himself out of sight from those on the roof. Danny peeked over and spotted the wrought-iron railing above the ledge. Lifting his body slightly upwards, Danny shifted his grip to the railing, keeping his body as low as possible. He could hear foreign-sounding angry voices, one of which seemed quite close by, and some sobbing. He cautiously lifted his head slightly so that he could see what was going on.

A dark-haired man in a suit, machine gun raised in one outstretched hand, was standing right there, facing a group of people sitting on the floor. His back was right up against the wrought-iron railing, about two inches from Danny's nose. Danny peeked from behind the man's back and made out two other men with guns, stationed at opposite ends of the observation area. One of them was standing a few feet away from some machine-like thing with wires and a blinking clock on it.

Nobody had noticed him yet, but Danny knew he could not count on his luck holding for long. His brain started kicking into overdrive to develop some kind of plan, but unfortunately, one of the tourists nearby spotted him and began pointing and waving excitedly.

The next few seconds seemed to happen in some kind of weird slow motion. The terrorist right in front of Danny turned his head around. Danny instinctively made a fist, smashed it through the iron bars of the railing and into the Jihadist's surprised face. The terrorist was thrown backward from the edge of the roof and crumpled to the floor in a heap. Ripped-out pieces of railing clattered noisily down all around the fallen gunman.

The other two Jihadists instantly trained their guns on Danny. After a quick nod at each other, one of them charged at him, yelling something incomprehensible and opening fire as he approached. The other turned and moved toward the bomb. Everyone on the roof began screaming, crying, or both. It was a full-on public panic attack.

Danny vaulted over the remains of the railing, bullets sparking off his body, and planted a foot in the chest of the onrushing terrorist. The Jihadist was sent hurtling across the roof, right into the path of the third terrorist. Danny watched, hoping for a lucky break, but the Jihadist saw his unconscious buddy coming and flattened himself to the floor. As the body crashed into the wall behind him, the remaining terrorist lunged forward, reaching out a hand for the yellow button next to the bomb clock.

Danny hurled himself across the deck as fast as he could, a desperate green streak trying to save his city. His body slammed into the third terrorist just as the man's hand made contact with the bomb. The Jihadist was tossed to the side like a bowling pin, fell to the floor and did not move.

All the terrorists were down! Mission accomplished! He had saved the city!

Then a familiar-looking cameraman walked up, pointed behind Danny and whispered in a frightened voice,

"Look."

Then he said it much louder, with deeply rooted fear. The dread penetrated everyone who heard it, including Danny. It was the voice of unstoppable, impending catastrophe.

"LOOK!!!"

Danny turned. He was not sure what the little red numbers on the bomb had read before, but now they showed:

00:00:09

He had doomed them all.

Only one option remained, and he did not have time to dwell on it. Before his eyes, one more second clicked away. He bent down, grabbed the bomb with both hands, and exploded into the air. He had to get this thing far enough away so that it would not hurt anyone. He had no idea if he was capable of that, but he would give it his best shot. Maybe he would even have time to save himself at the end.

More than a billion people around the world would bear live witness to happened next, all thanks to the alert camerawork of Benjamin Bowman, whose video stream was carried live on TV and over the internet. They would remember where they were at that moment for the rest of their lives.

In downtown Brooklyn, Mike Petersen and his loyal executives viewed it from the flat screen TV in Petersen's office. Most of the staff had long since gone home, but Petersen had stayed at his post, and his executives were intimidated enough to remain with him.

In Staten Island, Mr. Simonelli and Mugsy were in the mansion's den, with Bugsy peeking in from the hallway. The Mafia boss actually found himself hoping Pickle Boy would succeed. He did not want to see his city destroyed. Bad for business. Then he thought of the Voice, and shivered. Pickle Boy's death would definitely take some heat off him. Maybe losing Manhattan would not be so bad after all.

Joe and Sammy were sitting on Joe's bed. Joe knew his father did not approve of him bringing friends home, and he definitely didn't approve of Pickle Boy. Joe had a nice bruise on his face as proof of that. However, his father was currently drunk and passed out in his own room, and Joe had more to be concerned about right now. He and Sammy were online, their hearts in their throats, as they watched their best friend try to save them all.

Danny's mother had elected to remain at home at the end. She could not bear to leave both her son and husband behind. She clutched Miri on her lap, watching matters unfold, tears streaming from her face.

Shia Dekel did not really care, but had no choice but to

watch what was going on. His mother was trying to drive them out of Brooklyn, but they were stuck on the Belt Parkway with about a million other people. The TV in the car was tuned in, of course, to what was happening at the Empire State Building. His feeble brain was actually hoping for a nice big explosion. That would be kind of cool. Especially if it killed Pickle Boy.

Danny's father had gotten most of the way to the Manhattan Bridge on foot, but stopped when he saw a crowd of people gathered around the windows of an electronics store and the televisions on display there. He would not realize until later that it was his son that was preparing to sacrifice his life in an attempt to save New York.

Finally, there was Joseph Picolo, who peered with great trepidation through the bars in his cell at his guards' TV. He was concerned, of course, for all the New Yorkers who were in grave danger, but he was almost equally anxious about the fate of the brave boy in green. Pickle Boy represented the best hope against a looming danger even greater than nuclear terrorism. The world needed him to survive.

Benjamin kept his camera trained on Pickle Boy as he shot into the sky. The updraft created by Danny's extreme takeoff had almost knocked him off his feet, but he steadied himself by grabbing onto a busted section of railing that was still attached to the roof. Everyone on the observation deck, and indeed, everyone in the city who had been watching the action unfold on TV or online, turned their eyes skyward to follow Danny's flight. The millions of New Yorkers still in Manhattan knew that their very existence would be decided in the next few seconds. The time ticked off inside everyone's mental clocks as they watched and waited. Each second felt like years as the figure of the boy disappeared out of view, and then...

A second sun suddenly appeared in the sky high above the Empire State Building. People averted their eyes from the harsh glare, and many felt a surge of heat wash over them as well. The fireball remained visible for a few minutes, then dissipated. It was over! The boy had done it. He had done it!!!

The city erupted in hysterical celebration. It was like a walk-off grand slam to win the World Series, magnified a thousand times. New Yorkers of all sizes, shapes and colors, and people around the world as well, hugged and embraced each other with abandon. Captain Fazio was high-fiving every officer in reach, even the guy with the megaphone. The celebrations went on for several more minutes until a boy, who had been one of the hostages on the observation deck (now swarming with police and FBI personnel), tugged on his mother's arm and asked,

"What about Pickle Boy, Mommy? What happened to him? Is he coming back?"

Benjamin overheard his question and trained his camera toward the sky once again. "I'm looking, kid!" he shouted. "You look, too. I'm sure he's ok. He'd better be ok! It would really suck if…well, you know…"

The young newsman did not realize that the camera's mike was still on, and that his words were still being broadcast worldwide. The city quieted noticeably, as all eyes searched the heavens for clues as to what had happened to Pickle Boy.

Danny had simply flown straight upward, and had poured on as much speed as he possibly could. He willed his body ever higher and ever faster, shooting through the cloud layers and beyond, into the upper stratosphere. He did not stop until the sky around him was almost completely black, at which point he glanced down to see how far he had gotten.

The Northern Hemisphere was laid out in front of him, and it was the most beautiful thing he had ever seen. He could make out the great greenish land mass of North America directly below. It was almost the same color as his clothing. He could not believe he had gotten so high up! The city was probably safe. Now he could get rid of the bomb. And there were still two whole seconds left on the clock!

He reared back, just as if he were preparing to throw a football, and…

It turned out the terrorists had one last little surprise for anyone who attempted to defuse the bomb.

The clock was two seconds slow.

CHAPTER 11

STILL ALIVE?

Danny's father finally made it home around six o'clock that evening. He had walked over the Manhattan Bridge and into Brooklyn together with tens of thousands of others, and all of them were in the friendliest frame of mind of their lives. It was a long walk, but a great experience nevertheless. Complete strangers were reliving their shared experience with one another as if they were lifelong best friends. Almost everyone mentioned how tough and brave that Pickle Boy had been, how he had shown those terrorists that you don't mess with New York. This was usually followed by a hopeful look upwards, and then a moment or two of silence when the search was unsuccessful.

Mr. Green had tried to call home every few minutes, but the lines remained jammed. Even texting did not work. He had overheard somebody mentioning that the nuclear explosion might have knocked out the satellites – maybe that was it. He hoped his wife and children were not too worried about him.

Mr. Green entered his home expecting a nice warm family welcome. And he got one, from Miri, anyway, who screamed "DADDY!" and gave him a huge hug.

"Hey, kiddo!" exclaimed Mr. Green, clapping her on the

back. "Glad to see me, huh? Boy, do I have a story to tell you. Hey, where's Danny?"

He looked around for his son but his eyes got caught on his wife's face. On the expression of terrible loss and pain that hung there. He had seen that expression only once before, when her mother had died suddenly. A deep foreboding filled his heart. Where was Danny?

He sent Miri off for some extra Prince Caprico time on the computer, and then turned to his wife, who for some reason had burst into tears at the mention of the fairy tale Prince.

"Aliza, what's wrong? The terrorists were stopped, the bomb is gone, and I'm home. They just don't know what happened to Pickle Boy…"

His wife held up one hand, motioning for him to stop. She led him into their bedroom and locked the door.

Fifteen minutes later, an ashen-faced Mr. Green stumbled out. His life had just been turned inside out and upside down. Way down.

Miri was put to bed early that night. Her mommy had tucked her in and told her how Pickle Boy had saved her, Daddy and all the other people in the city. It should have been a happy story, but Mommy had not seemed very happy as she told it. Miri pulled her covers tight around her body and dwelled on this for a bit. Maybe Mommy was just worried about Danny, who had gone out to play and had not come home yet. She hoped Danny would be punished for that. Good for him. He was always doing dumb things like ignoring her, or drinking pickle juice, or…hey, wait. Pickle juice. She had seen Danny drink that gross stuff the other day. Ewww. But maybe Pickle Boy liked pickle juice too! And maybe she could be friends with him if she also drank pickle juice. Cool! Maybe she could try some of

Danny's...and that was her last thought before she drifted off into sleep.

About seven thirty that evening, Sammy and Joe arrived at the Green home. They were not sure whether Danny had told his father and mother the truth about Pickle Boy, but they had decided together that now was the time. It was only right that Danny's parents should know what happened to their son. However, as soon as Mr. Green opened the front door to Sammy's tentative knocking, Danny's friends could tell right away that he was fully aware of the situation. At the same time, Mr. Green realized that Danny's friends were on the same page as he was. Wordlessly, the three embraced, and the boys began bawling uncontrollably, Joe even more so than Sammy. Mr. Green found himself comforting them, and it provided him with some small measure of peace to do so.

Later that evening, the President of the United States addressed the nation.

"My fellow Americans. Today our country, and in particular, the brave citizens of New York City, came face to face with the greatest evil that exists in our world. A group of terrorist madmen, without any provocation, attempted to murder millions of our fellow citizens. It was only through the brave actions of one boy, a boy who has refused to reveal his identity or seek honor for himself, that this terrible plan was ultimately unsuccessful. This country will always owe a debt of gratitude to this remarkable young man, a debt which can never be fully repaid."

The President paused for a moment, and then continued, with a noticeable catch in his voice.

"Uh, I - I regret to inform you that as of the present time, the whereabouts of Pickle Boy are still unknown. It is unclear whether he was able to separate from the bomb before it detonated. I have tasked both NASA and the United States Air Force, along with the local law enforcement agencies of the state of New York, with a top-priority mission to locate Pickle Boy. Our most sincere hopes and prayers go out to his family and friends, whoever they may be."

The President paused again, glanced at his notes, and continued, pointing a finger toward the camera as he did so.

"Let me make one thing perfectly clear. Today, America was attacked with a weapon of mass destruction. That the attack failed is of no matter. Neither I, nor the members of this administration, will rest until those behind the attack are brought to justice. We will use any and all means necessary, including the use of our own nuclear weapons, to ensure that this country will not be subject to this threat ever again. Any nation or organization found to be providing assistance of any kind to the perpetrators of this evil will be treated in the same manner as the terrorists themselves.

G-d bless America, and good night."

Mr. Simonelli had invited all of "the boys" to join him at the mansion for a double celebration – the city surviving and the apparent death of the snotty kid who had caused them so much trouble. The boss was in a great mood. He embraced his men heartily and offered them drinks from his extensive and valuable private stash. The party was in full swing by the time the President's speech came on, and they all cheered when he announced that Pickle Boy was still unaccounted for.

Mr. Simonelli allowed himself to relax. Everything was finally going well. Then the unique chirping of the grey telephone in his office brought him quickly down to earth.

He closed the door to his office and steeled himself for the forthcoming phone call. What could this be about? Maybe the Voice was calling to share in the good news? He sat down, exhaled deeply, and picked up the receiver.

"YOU IDIOT."

"Huh?" was all the shaking Mafia boss could manage.

"I SUPPOSE A FEEBLE- MINDED MAN SUCH AS YOU WOULD ASSUME THAT HIS JOB IS DONE AT THIS POINT. IT IS NOT. NOT AT ALL! YOU MUST REDOUBLE YOUR EFFORTS. THE FORMULA MUST BE LOCATED AND SECURED BEFORE SOME OTHER FOOL GETS THEIR HANDS ON IT. RESUME THE SEARCH. IMMEDIATELY!! OR SUFFER THE EXTREMELY UNPLEASANT CONSEQUENCES OF CONTINUED FAILURE!!!"

A flash of blinding pain through his skull brought Simonelli to his knees. Gasping for breath, he waited a few moments, steadied himself, then threw open the door to his office.

The men turned their eyes to him as one and stopped their celebrating immediately. The expression on Simonelli's face drove their smiles and grins from their faces. Nothing else needed to be said. The party was over. There was much work to be done.

The bird's programming had been partially reset by the explosion in the Vault. Instead of returning to Dr. Picolo's current place of imprisonment, it had attempted to return to the place of its original creation. In its damaged condition, it had taken a long time to cover the slightly more than one hundred miles between Brooklyn and Ellenville, New York. The bird's solar-powered motors were struggling as dusk began to fall, and its sensors began searching for a place to settle down. It landed in the branches of a tree alongside Route 52, just five miles from Dr. Picolo's old laboratory, and prepared to shut itself down for the night.

Wait. The last sweep of the sensors in its eyes had picked up some strange readings from the sparse forest bordering the highway. The bird fluttered its one working wing and hopped from one tree to the next. The readings got stronger and more identifiable as the bird ventured further off the road and deeper into the thickening forest. It was unmistakable. Nuclear radiation.

The bird finally zeroed in on the source of the readings and perched in a tree overlooking a clearing, in the center of which was a freshly made hole in the ground about twenty feet across. Trees had been flattened around the hole for fifty feet in every direction. Some object had impacted here recently with tremendous force. Perhaps a meteor. However, that would not explain the radiation.

Closer inspection was warranted. The bird drifted down to the edge of the hole and peered in.

Something burned and blackened was curled up at the bottom. It was not all black, though. Traces of greenish streaks were visible, even in the deepening gloom. The bird's sensors shifted into the infrared to get a better reading….

It was a boy. A boy with burnt green clothing. All the bird's sensors lit up. It was the boy it had been tracking all along!

It was too bad. This was the one his master had sent him to follow. Unfortunately, this boy had surely ceased to function. All that radiation, plus the blast and the fall that he had obviously suffered through. Very unfortunate indeed.

The bird bowed its head as if in sorrow, and then turned away. His master would have to start his search again. Would they find their champion in time to face the coming evil? It now appeared very doubtful…

Then its sensors registered something. A faint energy spike. And the slightest of movements.

The bird turned back towards the boy.

The boy's eyes had opened.

EPILOGUE -

AND REVELATIONS

Despite Tommy's vehement protests, Uncle Dan had to stop his tale at this point, but allowed Tommy some time to ask questions.

It turned out that Tommy had a lot on his mind. Obviously, he wanted to know if Danny was going to survive, and if so, how badly the nuclear explosion had hurt him. He was also very curious about the identity of the mysterious "Voice", and what exactly was the looming threat that Dr. Picolo was so worried about. Uncle Dan reassured him that he would do his best to answer these questions when he returned from his vacation. Then, almost as an afterthought, Tommy wondered aloud about whatever happened to BlackJack. Uncle Dan appeared to be taken by surprise at this comment and his demeanor became much more serious.

"BlackJack. Funny you should mention him." Uncle Dan scratched his chin thoughtfully. "Well, he and his gang sort of avoided each other after he got beaten up by what they thought was just an average little kid. BlackJack had been publicly humiliated, and the gang, although they still feared their leader, felt uncomfortable around him. But BlackJack would eventually find a way to strike back at Danny, and he actually has quite a large role to play in Danny's future adventures. It's important that we get to that as soon as I get back."

"Whoa!" was all an open-mouthed Tommy could say. He had not been expecting such a detailed response to his offhand remark.

Uncle Dan headed for the door, but just as he was about to leave…

"Wait, Uncle Dan! Please, one last thing?"

"Yes, Tommy?

"Uncle Dan, you said that there really was a Pickle Boy, just everyone forgot about it."

"That's right, Tommy," said Uncle Dan with a mischievous smile.

"Come on. Are you really serious about this?" asked Tommy doubtfully.

"Why do you ask?"

"Because if it was like you say, that it's really a true story, just everyone forgot it…"

Tommy paused a bit, then asked triumphantly,

"So how do *you* know the story? Wouldn't you have forgotten it, too?"

Once again, Uncle Dan was caught off-balance.

"I, uh, me? How do I know the story. Well. How *do* I know the story? Good question, Tommy. Excellent. I'll have to let you think about that one."

"Hah! I knew it! You made the whole thing up, right, Uncle Dan?"

Uncle Dan just smiled. "We'll talk about this next time, Tommy. Goodbye!"

Uncle Dan headed downstairs to gather his things together before Tommy's parents got home. He was startled to find a man sitting on the couch. A man he recognized instantly, although he had not seen him in over twenty years. The man was holding a jar of sour pickles.

"Well, well," came the gruff but familiar voice. "Little Danny Green. Not so little anymore, I see. Still fond of these, Danny?" asked the Director of the FBI, extending the jar towards Dan. "I brought some, in case I needed to jog your memory."

Dan was too shocked to speak. He had known the man now sitting in his nephew's living room as FBI Agent David Gold, all those years ago. Now Mr. Gold was in charge of the whole Bureau and all of its secrets, but *his* secret was supposed to be safe from everyone, even the FBI. That was the deal Dan had made. He had given up everything, and had gotten his regular life back. Nevertheless, Agent, or rather, Director Gold had somehow managed to dig up the truth.

Uncle Dan felt the old panic rising up inside him, as it nearly always did when things seemed to get completely hopeless, but the Director's next words calmed him down somewhat.

"Danny, let me just say I am really sorry to surprise you like this, and truly mean you no harm. Far from it. Lord knows, you've done enough, and sacrificed enough, for all of us. And let me also reassure you that no one else in the world knows what I know."

"But how…?"

"Purely by accident. I was poking around in some of the agency's old computer files and came across something buried deep in the systems used to shelter sensitive records in case of nuclear attack. It's probably the only place on Earth where these records could have survived. Needless to say, once I began to read them, it all came back to me. All that had happened, and also how and why it all vanished from history. Needless to say, I made sure these records are accessible only to me, and will self-delete if anyone else tries to get at them."

Dan was still trying to process what he had just been told as the Director continued.

"I would have left you alone, knowing that you preferred it that way, but I felt it was my duty to make sure you had started telling the story to your nephew."

Dan Green finally found his normal voice. "I actually did, about a month ago. But why would you care…oh. Oh, no."

He spotted a calendar hanging on the wall. It was amazing how quickly the years had passed.

The Director understood that Dan had grasped what was at stake. "You know what you have to do, Danny. If you need anything, anything at all, please do not hesitate to call me at this number." The Director handed Dan a plain white business card with a series of ten digits printed in bold across the middle.

Director Gold placed the jar of pickles on a side table and stood up to leave.

"Danny, it's truly honor to meet you again. Make sure

the boy is prepared. I know you will do what has to be done. Just as you always have in the past."

The men shook hands, and the Director headed out towards his waiting car.

Dan sat down heavily on the couch. How could he have forgotten? Tommy had to be brought up to speed as soon as possible.

The full story of Pickle Boy needed to be told.

THE END...

FOR NOW!

ABOUT THE AUTHOR

The author, an experienced storyteller known only as "Jack Bee" has been verbally sharing the Awesome Adventures of Pickle Boy to selected groups of trusted individuals for several years. It is only now that he has reluctantly agreed to allow his work to be transcribed into written form. He has hinted that more material may be forthcoming, once public reaction to the publication of the first Volume has been properly measured. The trusted individuals mentioned above are very difficult to locate and have also been sworn to Absolute Secrecy, so there is little chance of more information about Pickle Boy being gleaned from them.

A reclusive individual who is obsessed with security, the author insists his real name not be used. He will neither confirm nor deny the truth of any of the events depicted in the Adventures, merely commenting that what the world believes is history is what it is allowed to believe.

Questions and comments relating to the Adventures may be directed to pickleboy613@yahoo.com. Mr. Bee promises to respond as long as the questioner (or any of his/her relatives) does not work for the FBI.

Mr. Bee has also hinted that the names of the chapters in this first volume of the Adventures have a hidden correspondence to an ancient book. He has agreed to come out of seclusion and personally deliver a container of sour pickles to the first one to guess and explain this correspondence to him, provided that this individual can make it to Brooklyn.

Mr. Bee reportedly resides in Brooklyn with his wife and six children. It is quite possible that one of them is named Miri.

Made in the USA
San Bernardino, CA
05 December 2018